Trouble at Lake Tahoe

Nancy shifted her position in the raft, searching for the nearest shore. But she and Katie were far out in the lake—they might have to swim for miles. Even worse, both of them were still weak, and the raft had no paddles.

Suddenly Nancy sat up straight, cocking her head.

"What is it?" Katie asked.

Nancy put her fingers to her lips, motioning Katie to be quiet. Then she heard it again—a faint hissing noise. She pressed her ear to the side of the raft. The sound became louder.

Slowly Nancy ran her hand along the side of the raft, then stopped. Katie watched her, not moving a muscle. The raft's smooth skin was broken by a small snag. Leaving her fingers on it, Nancy leaned over to look. Her heart sank.

The snag was actually a small tear, about an inch long. The raft had been punctured, and air was rapidly escaping.

Nancy and Katie were sinking!

Nancy Drew
Mystery Stories

Available from MINSTREL Books

118

NANCY DREW®

TROUBLE AT LAKE TAHOE

CAROLYN KEENE

A MINSTREL® BOOK

PUBLISHED BY POCKET BOOKS

New York   London   Toronto   Sydney   Tokyo   Singapore

A MINSTREL PAPERBACK *ORIGINAL*

 A Minstrel Book published by
POCKET BOOKS, a division of Simon & Schuster Inc.
1230 Avenue of the Americas, New York, NY 10020

Copyright © 1994 by Simon & Schuster Inc.

Produced by Mega-Books of New York, Inc.

ISBN: 0-671-79304-7

First Minstrel Books printing April 1994

10 9 8 7 6 5 4 3

Cover art by Aleta Jenks

Printed in the U.S.A.

Contents

TROUBLE AT LAKE TAHOE

1

Fun in the Sun

"Unbelievable!" George Fayne exclaimed, turning to her friend Nancy Drew. "Have you ever seen anything so beautiful?"

Nancy smiled and held up a hand to shield her blue eyes from the piercing sun. She followed her friend's gaze to the sparkling blue-green lake in front of them.

The endless clear water was met suddenly at its far edge by the towering Sierra Nevada mountains. Although it was late June, the evergreen-covered peaks were still capped by patches of white snow.

"No," Nancy said, dropping her hand and looking at George. "I don't think I *have* seen anything quite like Lake Tahoe."

"Everything is so clear," Bess Marvin added, rubbing some warmth into her bare arms.

1

Though the sun shone brightly overhead, at that altitude the morning air was still cool.

Before Nancy or George could reply, they were interrupted by a cheerful voice behind them. "Well, is it everything you imagined?" Nancy turned to the tall, lean young woman who approached them.

The young woman's brown hair, streaked blond by the sun, was pulled back in a ponytail, and her freckled face had a big smile on it. "I think seeing Lake Tahoe for the first time is like seeing one of the Seven Wonders of the World," the young woman said, casually throwing an arm around Nancy's shoulders.

"It is wonderful," Nancy agreed. "But, Katie, why aren't you taking a practice run?"

"Yeah," George chimed in, motioning toward the speedboats that dotted the lakeshore. "Most of the other water-skiers are out, practicing for the tournament."

Katie Cobb smiled. An old friend of Nancy's, she had moved from their hometown, River Heights, to Mission Bay, California, a few years before. Since then she had become one of the top water-skiers in the country. This week she was competing in a women's tournament at Lake Tahoe and had invited Nancy, Bess, and George to spend a few days with her at the mountain retreat.

The girls had flown into nearby Reno, Nevada, the previous night, then had driven to Incline Village, where they were renting a cabin. This morning they were having their first glimpse of Lake Tahoe and Sand Harbor, the beach where the three-day tournament would be held.

Katie smiled at George. "I took my practice run half an hour ago," she said.

"But your hair isn't wet," Bess pointed out.

"That shows I had a good practice run." Katie grinned. "I didn't fall—unlike those girls." She gestured toward the lake.

Nancy laughed as she took in the two skiers, who were peeling off their black, rubbery wetsuits and wringing out their hair.

The tournament was scheduled to begin in about an hour, and spectators were trickling down to the beach from the parking lot. Above the sounds of water lapping against the shore and speedboats taking off, Nancy could hear people calling to one another.

The beach had been set up as a temporary boat launch area. Coarse sand, about fifty yards wide, stretched along the curving edge of the lake. A long wooden dock jutted out into the water from the middle of the beach. Just past the dock an asphalt drive ran down from the parking lot to the water's edge. Nancy watched as a car backed its trailer and boat into the water for launching.

At the opposite end of the beach a tent had

been set up. A large banner over it read: Far West Regional Waterskiing Championship. Nearby, a wooden lifeguard tower was to be used as a judges' stand.

People were scattered about the beach, some clustered around the tent and some beside the shore. Others were carefully selecting just the right spot on the beach to watch the tournament and enjoy the sun.

Nancy brushed a strand of reddish blond hair back from her face. "Do you expect a big crowd?" she asked Katie, without turning.

Katie shrugged. "Not too big," she said. "It's still early in the season, and this is only a regional championship. Waterskiing tournaments are generally pretty casual. There will be some sports reporters around, mostly from local papers. I did hear that the ASC—the All-Sports Channel—sent a camera crew to get some footage."

Bess, who had been arranging her towel on the sand, hopped up suddenly. "You mean you'll be on TV?" she asked excitedly.

Katie's ever-ready grin stretched across her tanned face. "Maybe—if I ski well," she said. "But I'm just hoping to make a good showing here. It's my first time in the overall competition."

"Overall?" Bess asked.

"There are three events in tournament skiing," Katie explained, "slalom, trick, and jump. A skier can compete in as many of the events as she wants to. I used to compete only in slalom."

"That's where you put both feet on one ski and weave around a series of buoys," George explained to Bess.

Katie nodded. "Right. In the trick competition you perform a routine with lots of fancy moves. And in the jump event you ski up a ramp and see how far you can fly through the air before you hit water again."

Bess shuddered. "Sounds dangerous to me!" George laughed at Bess's reaction. Although the two eighteen-year-old girls were cousins, dark-haired George was an athlete and loved all sports, while blond, blue-eyed Bess preferred less demanding activities, such as shopping.

"It is dangerous, until you learn how to do it right," Katie agreed. "But I've been working hard on my jumping and my trick routine, and now I feel ready to compete in all three events. I think about a dozen of us are competing for the overall title."

"How is the winner chosen?" Nancy asked as they sat down on their towels.

"We start out with a field of sixteen in each event," Katie explained. "Each event is scored differently, but by tomorrow the field will be cut in half, which leaves only eight competitors in each event. On the third day—the final day of the tournament—it will be cut to four people in each. The winner of the overall title has the best average score in all three events."

"And that'll be you," Bess said, bobbing her head confidently. "I just know it."

"I hope you're right." Katie paused, taking a deep breath. "But it won't be easy." She pointed to a girl unzipping her water-ski bag by the shore. Her blond hair was pulled back in a tight French braid. "That's Pam Cartwright. She's going for the overall title, too. And she's done really well in the past couple of tournaments."

"She looks pretty young," Nancy noted.

Katie grimaced. "I know," she said. "She's only seventeen—the youngest skier in the tournament. And she only gets better and better." Then Katie's face brightened suddenly. She stood up and cupped her hands around her mouth. "Jackie!" she called, standing up.

Nancy saw a short, dark-haired young woman near the shore turn her head toward them. She smiled and waved, then began to walk over.

She was wearing a white windbreaker over a striped swimsuit. Noticing her muscular legs, Nancy knew she had to be a water-skier.

"All set?" the young woman said to Katie as she reached the group.

"I hope so," Katie said. "Jackie Albert, I want you to meet my friends from River Heights— Nancy Drew, George Fayne, and Bess Marvin." The girls shook hands with Jackie. "You've got to

6

watch Jackie in the trick division," Katie went on. "She's the best. She taught me my first tricks years ago."

Jackie smiled modestly. "And I'd say you're a pretty fast learner—you had a great practice run this morning. It's a good thing we're not competing against each other for the overall. I'm glad I'm just entered in trick."

"Jackie and I practice together when we're at tournaments," Katie explained to the others. "We've been in so many tournaments together that we know each other's skiing pretty well by now."

Jackie ran a hand through her short hair and glanced at the tournament tent nervously. "I hate to run," she said, "but I still need to check in, and, Katie, the slalom event is about to start."

"That means it's time for me to get going," Katie said. "Wish me luck!"

Nancy gave Katie a hug. "You'll hear us cheering you on," she said.

"It was nice meeting all of you," Jackie said with a goodbye wave. After she and Katie walked away, Bess turned to Nancy and George. "Katie's as energetic as ever, isn't she?" she said.

George nodded. "And pretty calm, too. No wonder she's a top water-skier. She seems so focused, even with all the pressure. I hope she'll have time to give me some skiing pointers."

Bess stretched out on her towel. "All I want to

focus on is lying here in the sunshine," she said with a smile.

"How about a compromise?" Nancy suggested. "Let's first move closer to the shore so we can get a good view of Katie's slalom round, then soak up some rays." Nancy slung her blue- and white-striped beach bag over her shoulder and led the way down to the water's edge.

Several people were walking up and down the long dock; others were sitting on the edges. On the beach spectators stood in groups or sat in beach chairs, waiting for the slalom competition to start. The sand sloped down toward the water, providing a natural grandstand view of the action on the lake.

"Is slalom in waterskiing like slalom in snow skiing?" Bess asked as they settled down on the shore. "I've seen snow slaloming on TV. The skiers maneuver around poles stuck in the snow."

George nodded. "It's the same, but in waterskiing, they weave around those orange buoys," she said, pointing to two rows of buoys bobbing in the lake a few hundred feet off the shore. "The motorboat pulls the skier between the rows, and the skier swings out to either side to go around the buoys."

"But if the skier is being pulled by a rope attached to a boat, doesn't the rope get in the way?" Bess frowned.

"It's easier with a long rope," George said.

"But with each round the competitors use shorter and shorter ropes, even though the buoys are still the same distance apart. It gets more and more difficult—the skier really has to stretch her body to make it around a buoy."

"How do you know so much about water-skiing?" Nancy asked.

George shrugged. "I've skied a few times and seen it on television, too," she said. "It's not easy. I can't wait to see this competition up close."

"Now's your chance," Nancy said, motioning to the lake. "There goes Katie!" She watched through her binoculars as a sleek, spotlessly clean powerboat pulled Katie toward the slalom area.

Katie seemed so poised as she leaned back on her ski, ready to begin her run. The ski skimmed over the sparkling water, and Katie almost seemed to be flying across its surface.

"Our first competitor is Katie Cobb," a voice announced over a loudspeaker. The spectators on shore grew silent as Katie approached the first buoy. Bess grabbed Nancy's arm. "Look how fast she's going," she said excitedly.

Nancy nodded. She could feel her heart begin to race as Katie swung easily in a curve around the first buoy. The boat sped forward in a straight line down the center of the double line of buoys. Katie had to pull the rope from side to side in order to wind around the buoys.

Approaching the second one, Katie positioned

her ski to go around the neon orange buoy and leaned over the buoy sideways, holding the rope with one hand. The ski cut around the buoy smoothly, and Katie straightened up as she headed for the next one.

"She's doing great!" George exclaimed. "Her form is perfect."

As Nancy watched, Katie took the next three buoys almost effortlessly. The boat sped through the water, and Katie sent up a wall of spray as she cut back and forth.

Heading for the sixth and last buoy, she swung her weight around, pulling the rope toward the orange marker. She positioned her ski again and leaned in toward the buoy.

In a split second, though, the ski shot out from under her. A huge funnel of water from the splash could be seen from the shore as the rope jerked out of Katie's hands.

Katie had disappeared beneath the surface!

2

Tricks Can Be Dangerous

Nancy took a deep breath and kept her eyes glued to the sixth orange buoy. Short intakes of air were the only sounds heard from the spectators as they realized Katie had fallen.

"Oh, no!" Bess cried out in dismay. "Where is she?"

The crowd's tense silence was broken by a collective sigh of relief as Katie's head popped up above the water. Bobbing along in her life vest, she waved to the shore to indicate that she was all right.

"Thank goodness she's okay," George said. "But what a shame. She was doing so well."

Bess nodded. "I wonder what happened," she said.

Nancy shook her head. "Whatever it was, I'm

sure it's not the way Katie wanted to begin the tournament."

Nancy turned her head, and her eye was caught by some movement on the long dock that stretched into the lake. She saw a woman running to the end of the dock. The woman was tall and lean, and her light brown hair was pulled back in a low ponytail. She waved urgently at Katie. Katie, who was putting her ski back on as she bobbed in the water, waved back.

Nancy turned to Bess and George. "That's Katie's mother," she said. "I'm going to go say hello." She walked over to the woman.

At the end of the dock Katie's mother stood nervously with her arms crossed, watching Katie. "Mrs. Cobb?" Nancy said, stepping up to her.

The tall woman turned to Nancy and her expression remained blank for a moment. Then her face broke out in a smile. "Nancy Drew!" she said brightly. "My goodness, how you've grown." Mrs. Cobb held her arms out and gave Nancy a big hug. "How's your father?" she asked. Nancy's father, Carson Drew, was a well-known River Heights attorney.

"He's fine, thank you," Nancy answered.

"I was looking for you earlier," Mrs. Cobb said. "Katie said you and your friends arrived last night."

Nancy nodded and smiled. "We rented a cabin at Incline Village."

"Close to ours, I hope," Mrs. Cobb replied. Then the smile left her face. "I just wish Katie had had a better start this morning," she said, shaking her head.

She peered over Nancy's shoulder. Nancy turned to see Katie emerging out of the water in her dripping wet life vest. Her expression was grim.

Mrs. Cobb pulled a towel out of her shoulder bag to hand to Katie when she joined them on the dock. "What happened?" she asked. "Did you lean too far?"

Katie shook her head in frustration as she took off the vest and wrapped the towel around herself. "No," she said firmly. "That wasn't it."

"Maybe you just miscalculated a bit going into the turn," her mother began. "Remember—"

"I remember," Katie interrupted. "I know that I've done that before. But not this time. The whole course felt different this time," she said, her attention on the lake. "It felt like the ski was trying to slip away from me." Katie became lost in thought for a moment.

Nancy turned to Mrs. Cobb with a grin. "You sound like you could be Katie's coach."

Mrs. Cobb smiled modestly. "I *am* Katie's coach," she said. "I took over recently. I did some exhibition skiing years ago—*many* years ago," she added wryly.

"It wasn't *that* many," said a deep voice behind

13

them. Nancy saw a tall, dark-haired man with a video camera approach. His eyes twinkled, and he had the same wide grin as Katie. Nancy recognized him as Bruce Cobb, Katie's father.

"Nice try, sweetheart," he said to Katie, giving her a kiss on the cheek.

Katie rolled her eyes and said, "Dad, you remember Nancy Drew, don't you?"

"River Heights's most famous amateur detective? Of course I do," Mr. Cobb said, shaking Nancy's hand. "Katie has told us about some of the mysteries you've solved."

Before Nancy could respond, another voice from behind Mr. Cobb piped up, "Maybe she can figure out why Katie wiped out." As Mr. Cobb stepped aside, Nancy saw a smaller, younger version of Katie standing on the dock. Her long hair was darker than Katie's, but she had the same freckled face and green eyes.

"You must be Bridget," Nancy said, smiling. "But I know you don't remember me. You were pretty little when I last saw you."

Bridget shook her hand and asked, "Well, do you want to take on 'The Case of Katie's Collapse'?"

"Bridget, it was only a slight mistake," Mrs. Cobb said, frowning at the younger girl. "Besides, everything depends on how Anna DeRicco does—she skis next." Katie's mom turned to Nancy and explained, "The slalom is a head-to-head competition—Katie is paired with another skier, in this case Anna DeRicco. Whichever of them successfully skis around the most buoys advances to the next round."

Bess and George walked up to the group at the end of the dock, and Nancy introduced the cousins to the Cobbs. Then they all turned to watch Anna DeRicco begin her slalom run.

Nancy could see Katie's body grow tense as she watched Anna round the first few buoys in perfect form. Mrs. Cobb put an arm around Katie as Anna came around the fourth buoy. But Anna jerked around the marker unsteadily. As she wobbled into her approach for the fifth buoy, she completely lost her balance and fell.

Katie dropped her clasped hands and sighed in relief. Mrs. Cobb's face relaxed a bit, too. Katie had skied past one more buoy than Anna had, so she would compete in the next day's round.

"Now let's forget about slalom until tomorrow," Mrs. Cobb said to Katie as they walked back down the dock toward the beach. "It's time to start focusing on trick."

Following her mom, Katie called back to Nancy, "I'll catch up with you guys after the trick round, okay?"

"We have a big umbrella set up on the beach," Mr. Cobb said to Nancy and her friends as they walked off the dock. "You girls are welcome to join us there. But if you want to get the best view of the trick, you should move down to the far end of the beach."

"What happens in trick?" Bess asked Mr. Cobb.

"It's a lot of fun," Katie's father began. "The skiers wear a small ski that allows them to maneuver more easily. They do spins, turns, and twists. They've got ninety seconds to perform as many tricks as they can. But they're also scored on the difficulty of each individual trick."

"Who assigns the scores?" Nancy asked.

"There are two judges on the shore, and a third who rides in each competitor's boat," Mr. Cobb explained. He pointed to a man and woman in orange windbreakers standing at the far end of the beach. "So the skiers try to give each trick individual flourishes." He patted his video camera. "I need to grab another blank tape. We'll meet you girls at the far end of the beach. Coming, Bridget?" Bridget shrugged and followed her father.

Left to themselves Nancy, Bess, and George began to walk down the beach. The sun was almost directly overhead now, and the sand was becoming hot to the touch. Bess removed her sandals and walked into the water. "Whoa!" she cried, and stepped back on the sand. "No wonder those skiers move so fast in the water," she said. "It's too cold to stay in there long."

George studied her cousin. "Maybe you'd be

interested in skiing a little yourself," she suggested.

Bess shook her head emphatically. "No way," she declared. "A canoe is more my speed."

George laughed and turned to Nancy. "Did you find out what happened during Katie's run?"

"Not really," Nancy said. "Katie doesn't think she miscalculated the course. But she felt very unsteady during the whole run and doesn't know why."

"I hope the trick run goes well for her," George said.

Nancy nodded. "Me, too," she agreed. They joined the group already gathered at the end of the beach, near a large outcropping of rocks that extended into the lake. Nancy, Bess, and George made their way to an open spot in front.

"Isn't that Jackie Albert?" Bess asked, pointing to the skier being pulled across the lake. She was standing, in a crouched position, on a short ski.

"That's her," Nancy said. Several people in the small crowd were clapping and yelling encouragement to Jackie. Nancy watched the boat pick up some speed, and then Jackie suddenly spun around in a complete circle, rotating her hands rapidly over the rope handle. The spectators applauded. Jackie swiftly pulled the rope behind her and wrapped it around her waist. Then she spun out of the rope, whipping around in a flash.

"Wow!" Nancy said. "Katie was right. Jackie *is*

good." She watched as Jackie attached her foot to a holster in the rope, freeing her hands. With one foot in the ski and the other holding the rope, Jackie twisted around backward. After a series of spins and jumps, she turned back around, dropped her foot from the holster, and grabbed the rope handle with her hands again.

Then Jackie skidded her ski up onto the wake, the trail of choppy water left behind the moving boat. Using the wake as a little ramp, she flipped head over heels, landing firmly on her ski. The crowd roared.

A buzzer sounded, signaling the end of Jackie's ninety seconds. Nancy saw the Cobbs walking toward her. Mrs. Cobb was obviously worried. "Katie's next, and she's got her work cut out for her, I'm afraid."

Bess turned to Mrs. Cobb. "How did Jackie hold on to the rope with her feet?" she asked in awe.

"The rope is specially made for trick skiing with a foot holster built in," Mrs. Cobb explained. "It's a little tricky—if you need to let go for some reason, you can't just drop the rope, the way you can when you're holding it with your hands. But there's a release mechanism on the boat—if a skier falls, the rope is released from the boat. Katie has several foot tricks in her routine, too."

"Here she goes!" Mr. Cobb said, nudging his wife and lifting the video camera to his shoulder.

Nancy watched as Katie flew across the lake on the small ski. As the boat passed by, Nancy saw three people in it. She leaned toward Mrs. Cobb. "Who's in the boat besides the driver and the judge?" she asked.

"That's the observer," Mrs. Cobb said. "In trick you want to have someone watch the skier to make sure everything goes smoothly. Many of the moves are complicated. That's Tinker Clarkston out there. He's an old friend of ours and a real skiing pro." Squinting, Nancy saw he was a big man with a head of sun-bleached hair.

As Mrs. Cobb finished speaking Katie began her trick sequence. She led off with several of the same tricks that Jackie had done, twisting and spinning with the rope. Then she pulled the rope behind her, pushed it down toward the water, and jumped over it as if she were jumping rope. The spectators yelled and applauded.

After doing a backward flip keeping her body perfectly straight, Katie went right into her next jump: a leap from one side of the wake to the other. The jump was flawless, and the crowd began cheering loudly.

"So far, so good," Mrs. Cobb said, never taking her eyes off Katie. "Her movements are very controlled."

19

Nancy nodded and stared through her binoculars. Even to her untrained eye she could tell that Katie's tricks were more complicated and her moves more precise than Jackie's had been.

Katie moved the rope handle to her foot and turned backward. She spun around a few times with ease, carefully balancing herself. Mrs. Cobb drew in her breath. "Just a few seconds left," she murmured, checking her watch. "She should be going into her last trick."

Nancy's eyes were riveted on Katie as the skier turned back to face forward. Steadying herself, she leaned over her bent uplifted leg toward the rope holster. As she was about to release her foot, her ski hit a wave. The ski jerked out from under her, dropping Katie into the water.

Nancy saw Tinker Clarkston lean over and pull the automatic rope release. Nothing seemed to happen. As the force of the water thrashed around Katie's body, her foot remained trapped in the holster.

"Someone help her!" Mrs. Cobb screamed. "She'll be killed!"

3

At the End of Her Rope

Cries from the spectators rose as Katie was dragged along the lake. Tinker Clarkston whirled around in the speedboat to shout at the driver to stop. Then he whipped out a pocketknife and cut through the rope that was towing Katie.

She bounced one final time before stopping. Nancy watched as her body lay completely still on the water's surface, supported by her life vest. The driver of the boat had slowed down and made the sharp turn to go back to pick up Katie.

Nancy glanced to her right and saw that Mrs. Cobb's face had paled. "What happened?" the woman kept repeating to herself. "Tinker was pulling on the trick release, but the rope didn't budge."

Mr. Cobb had an arm around his wife, and the two of them were focused only on their daughter.

21

The boat circled close to Katie, and Tinker leaned over the stern to help her. He held out his hand, and Katie reached for it. Her mother gasped—Katie was all right. The crowd began to cheer when they saw Katie's hand move to give a feeble wave to the crowd.

With Tinker's help Katie made it back into the boat. Nancy thought Katie looked shaken but uninjured. "I'm sure she's fine," Nancy said, reassuring Mr. and Mrs. Cobb.

Mrs. Cobb gave Nancy a weak smile. "Thank you, dear. Let's go find out." She and Mr. Cobb quickly pushed their way through the spectators toward the boat landing area. Nancy, Bess, and George followed. Nancy noticed for the first time that Bridget had been behind them all the time and now followed along silently.

As they approached the stretch of beach marked off as the landing area, Katie's boat was gliding into shore. The driver had turned off the engine, and Tinker jumped into the shallow water to help guide the boat so that it could drop anchor. He caught sight of Mr. and Mrs. Cobb. "I think she's okay," he told them. "She's a tough little competitor."

"Thank goodness you were there, Tinker," Mrs. Cobb said as she ran to the side of the boat. Katie stood up and her mother helped her out of the boat, greeting her with a warm hug. "Are you all right?" Mrs. Cobb asked Katie. She held her daughter's face in her hands, peering anxiously into her eyes.

Katie nodded. She looked pale and tired. "My leg hurts," she said, "but I don't think anything is broken, just sore."

"Thank goodness for that," Bess blurted out. "I was so scared watching you."

"I was pretty scared, too," Katie said, managing a smile. "I've never had that happen before. I don't know what could have gone wrong with that release rope."

"It was stuck," Tinker said, shaking his head helplessly. "I pulled and pulled, but nothing happened."

The driver of the boat hopped out. "We used the same rope and release mechanism yesterday," he said, "and it was fine." He began to walk up the beach. "I'm going to report this to the tournament director." He gave Katie a reassuring pat on the shoulder and took off after the boat judge, who was already heading for the tent.

Nancy glanced quickly at George, who nodded, reading Nancy's thoughts exactly. "I'll go with you," George called to the driver, following him up the beach.

Nancy heard tiny splashes behind her and saw Jackie Albert running through the shallow water toward the group. She ran right up to Katie and grabbed her friend's hand.

"Are you okay?" she asked. Katie smiled and

nodded, and Jackie let out a deep breath. "I've never seen anything like that," she said. "I couldn't believe my eyes."

Mr. Cobb put his arm around his daughter. "You need to sit down," he said, leading Katie up onto the beach. Mrs. Cobb, Jackie, and Bridget followed, heading for the Cobbs' beach umbrella.

Bess started after them, but Nancy pulled her back. "I'd like to stay here and look around for a minute," she said in a low voice.

Bess looked surprised. "Why? What—" She caught herself, and her eyes grew round. Leaning toward Nancy, she asked, "You think this wasn't an accident?"

Nancy raised an eyebrow and shrugged. Then she turned to look in the boat. A steel bar protruded from inside the back of the boat. Nancy knew this was the tow bar to which the skier's rope was fastened.

Near the top of the bar a hook was attached to a steel mechanism. Nancy could see that the rope should have slipped right through the hook when Katie fell. Hanging from one end was a piece of the nylon rope, now frayed where Tinker had cut it.

On the side of the mechanism hung the small rope Tinker had pulled to activate the release. The mechanism had never released the rope from the hook.

Tinker still stood in the water by the side of the boat, watching Nancy examine the tow bar. "I've never seen anything like that," he commented. "The rope should have sprung right out when I pulled." He shook his head, baffled.

Nancy frowned. "Do these release ropes malfunction often?" she asked the older man.

Tinker was almost startled. "I've never heard of one doing it—ever," he said. "Especially not on the boats they use for tournaments. The tournament sponsors provide top-of-the-line equipment for skiers, so they can show off their products."

Nancy nodded slowly, thinking. Then Tinker waded over closer. "To tell the truth," he said, lowering his voice, "it'd be pretty unusual for a piece they just tested yesterday to suddenly jam." He paused for a moment. "I think somebody would have had to fiddle with it."

Nancy studied the man's tanned and lined face. Tinker had spoken the words she had just been thinking. She knew there was a slight possibility that the release rope had simply failed, but Katie, Jackie, and Tinker had all said that would be unusual.

Bess, standing a few feet away, had overheard the conversation. "Wasn't Katie's fall in the slalom unusual, too?" Bess asked.

Nancy checked Tinker before nodding. "I was

thinking the same thing. Maybe there's more to Katie's accidents than bad luck," she said uneasily.

She was startled to see a man standing near them. He was about Nancy's height and had dark, thinning hair. He seemed to be watching Nancy intently. When she stared back at him, he whipped around and moved off a bit.

Nancy turned back to Bess and Tinker. "Let's take a quick look inside the boat," she suggested. "Then we can join the others." She hoisted herself up and over the side of the boat.

The interior of the new blue-and-white speedboat was clean, furnished only with the driver's seat and two other seats that faced the rear of the boat. The engine was housed in a large square box in the middle of the boat. Long narrow storage bins ran the length of the boat on both sides.

Nancy checked out the bins. Because the boat was new, they were practically empty. She poked through, finding an extra safety flag, an oar, and a fire extinguisher.

To be thorough, she felt around the back of the bin. There was nothing in the first one, but in the second, her hand brushed something. She pulled it out, a crumpled, rubbery object. Unfolding it, she saw it was a black ski glove with a pink neon stripe at the wrist and forefinger.

She turned to Tinker. "Have you seen this before?" she asked, showing him the glove.

He shook his head. "It's not Katie's," he said. "She always wears red gloves. It's her trademark." He looked at the glove more closely. "But someone's been using this one—that's why it's wrinkled. It's a popular brand, but no one in our boat was wearing it today."

Nancy nodded thoughtfully, putting the glove in her pocket. She'd find out whose glove it was—and why it was in the boat.

Nancy next turned her attention to the tow bar. She bent down to check the hook hanging from the metal piece near the top of the bar. She slid her finger through the hook, gently pulling. The hook moved slightly before sticking. She did it again, turning her head. As she did she noticed something glinting in the sunlight.

Peering closely at the hook, she examined the square piece of metal holding it. Two small rods held the hook and the release device. Jammed between them was a straight pin the size of a small hatpin.

Nancy reached in and, with a couple of sharp tugs, pulled the pin out. She held it up to Tinker, who was peering over her shoulder. "I don't think this is part of the mechanism, is it?" she asked. Tinker stared at the pin and shook his head gravely.

Nancy then grabbed the few inches of rope attached to the hook. When she jerked the rope, it snapped away from the hook easily.

Bess, still standing in the shallow water, drew in her breath. "Someone deliberately wedged a pin in there?" she said in disbelief. "But why? Katie could have been seriously hurt."

Nancy stood up with the pin in her hand. "I don't know," she said quietly. Her mind was racing. The pin must have been placed in the mechanism in order to jam it. If the rope had worked the day before, as the driver said, someone must have put the pin there more recently.

Nancy considered whether this could have been an act of general sabotage against the tournament. Katie was the first skier scheduled to use that boat in the trick event—and Nancy was still unsure if Katie's fall in the slalom was an accident or not. It looked as if someone were trying to hurt Katie. But Bess's question echoed in Nancy's head: Why?

"Listen, I'd like to go check on Katie," Tinker said, glancing up at the Cobbs' beach umbrella. Nancy snapped back to attention and nodded. Putting the pin in her pocket along with the glove, she stepped out of the boat and followed Bess and Tinker up the beach.

She had fallen a few yards behind when Nancy heard a deep voice behind her yell, "Hey!"

She whirled around and saw the same dark-haired man who had been staring at her before. He was at the water's edge, eyeing Nancy suspiciously. She frowned. "Excuse me?" she said abruptly.

"Who do you think you are?" the man demanded.

"Excuse me?" Nancy repeated.

"Who are you, snooping around like that?" the man said again, jerking his chin at Nancy. His arms were folded across his chest, and he was looking around nervously.

"Who are *you*?" Nancy retorted.

After deciding whether or not to answer her, he said in a voice full of authority, "I'm Gary Trachok, Pam Cartwright's coach."

Nancy blinked. The name seemed familiar, but she didn't know why. "I'm Nancy Drew," she said. "I'm a friend of Katie Cobb."

Trachok muttered, "It's too bad about her fall."

Nancy nodded slowly, wondering what Trachok might know about the fall. Before she could say anything, though, he took a step forward, thrusting his face right in front of hers.

"I know who messed with that release device," he declared, the words coming out in a rush.

Nancy backed away in surprise, but Trachok stepped even closer to her. Checking the beach furtively, he whispered hoarsely, "It was her sister—Bridget Cobb!"

4

Jumping to Conclusions

Nancy stood still, shocked by Trachok's statement. Then she stepped back from the man, still trying to put some space between them.

Why would Trachok accuse Bridget? And how did he know that the release mechanism was jammed, anyway? Nancy opened her mouth to speak, but Trachok cut her off.

"That's right—Bridget. Don't look so surprised, Ms. Drew. If you're really a friend of the family, then you know how nutty they all are. Sarah Cobb is no coach, and Bridget . . . well, let's just say Bridget would love to spoil things for her older sister. I'm sure tampering with the release rope is just her way of getting even with Katie after all the—"

Trachok stopped in midsentence. Nancy

30

turned to find Bess and George standing behind her, staring at the man in surprise.

Trachok muttered to Nancy, "Don't say I didn't warn you." Then he turned and began walking rapidly away from them.

George came to Nancy's side. "What was that all about?" she asked.

Nancy shook her head rapidly, as if to rid herself of Trachok's ominous speech. "I'm not sure," she said slowly, "but obviously he's not too fond of the Cobbs." She told George about finding the pin and then explained to her and Bess who Trachok was and what he had said.

Bess frowned. "It's not enough that Katie could have been killed," she said angrily, "now people want to blame her family for it! Who does this Trachok think he is?"

George turned to Nancy. "I hate to interrupt," she said, "but the Cobbs are waiting for us. They invited us to their cabin for lunch before the jump round this afternoon."

"Oh, yeah," Bess said, remembering. "They asked us to follow them in our car. It's just a short drive." Nancy nodded and the three began walking up the beach.

"What did the tournament director say?" Nancy said, asking George for an update.

"He was pretty upset," George reported. "He said the equipment would be checked out, but he agreed with the driver—the release mechanism and the rope were in perfect condition yesterday."

Nancy kept her head down, thinking.

"The one piece of good news," George added, "is that Katie had a terrific score on her trick run, even with her fall. She's leading the other competitors so far."

Nancy smiled. "That *is* good news."

After the intense sun on the beach, the Cobbs' rented cabin felt wonderfully cool. Nancy, Bess, and George were seated around a large wooden table with the Cobbs, eating turkey sandwiches and potato salad. The small A-frame cabin, decorated with Old West memorabilia, was cozy, and Nancy could tell that Mr. and Mrs. Cobb were starting to relax. Bridget remained quiet, picking at her food.

Half an hour after they finished eating, Katie sat on the floor to stretch. Nancy didn't want to upset Katie or her parents by telling them about the pin, but she had to clear up some questions in her mind. She turned to face Katie. "What do you know about Pam Cartwright's coach?" she asked.

Katie jerked her head up, surprised. Mr. and Mrs. Cobb glanced at each other and then stared at Nancy. "Why do you ask?" Katie replied.

Nancy shrugged. "He introduced himself to

me today, and I thought his name sounded familiar, that's all," she said casually.

Katie resumed stretching. "Gary Trachok used to be my coach," she said matter-of-factly.

Nancy put her hand to her head. "That's it," she said, finally making the connection. "I think you told me his name once, but I'd forgotten."

"I hope Trachok didn't bother you, Nancy," Mr. Cobb said sternly.

Nancy could tell this was a touchy subject with the Cobbs. She tried to downplay the incident. "I just wanted to place the name," she said.

"Well, we fired him only recently," Katie said from the floor. "When I started winning some tournaments, Gary decided I had a real shot at getting a national ranking. So he started to push me hard—too hard."

"He had her skiing constantly," Mrs. Cobb put in. "She did improve, but at what a cost. He kept her on too strict a training regimen, and he lectured her day and night."

"That's not my style," Katie went on. "I ski because it's fun, and I like to compete. But skiing isn't my whole life."

Nancy heard Bridget let out a short, sarcastic laugh.

Katie turned to her sister. "I know you think I'm obsessed with skiing, Bridget," Katie said. "But it really isn't my whole life—not anymore."

Nancy hesitated a moment and then asked, "What was Trachok's reaction to being fired?"

"He wasn't happy," Katie said grimly. "He told me it was my decision if I wanted to throw away a skiing career, but deep down I think he was angry and hurt." She thought for a moment. "Gary's a good coach, and Pam is doing well with him. But his regimen was too much for me."

"We tried to explain to Gary that we were afraid that Katie would get injured with those intense workouts," Mrs. Cobb added. "But he never really understood. We try to be civil toward him, but our relationship is not what you'd call friendly."

Nancy nodded. From what Trachok had said about the Cobbs that morning, Nancy had guessed that he didn't feel very friendly toward them. But now she wondered just how far his anger would go. Would it lead him to try to hurt Katie or sabotage her performance? He certainly was curious about Nancy's investigation of the trick rope release.

"Well," Mr. Cobb began, standing up to clear the table, "it's not Gary Trachok I'm worried about. I just hope that the tournament director finds out what was wrong with the release rope before another skier is hurt."

George and Bess focused on Nancy. She knew they were wondering if she would tell the Cobbs about the pin she had found. Nancy gave a brief shake of her head. She would tell the Cobbs eventually, but she didn't want to upset them any more now—Katie still had another round of skiing ahead of her that afternoon.

Suddenly Bridget spoke up. "It'd be easy to jam one of those release ropes," she said casually. "All you'd have to do is, like, stick a rod or pin or something in the hook part."

Nancy could feel her expression change as she heard Bridget. Was Bridget just guessing? Or was there some truth to what Gary Trachok had said—was it Bridget who had jammed the release?

"That could be," Mr. Cobb said to Bridget. "But why would anyone do it?"

Bridget shrugged and began to pull her long hair into a ponytail. Nancy stared at the girl, waiting for an answer. None came.

"I'd hate to think of someone doing that on purpose," Mrs. Cobb said, glancing at Katie worriedly. She got up and helped Mr. Cobb clear away the lunch dishes. "We'd better get going. We have to be back at the beach in time for the jump round."

As Nancy stood to help clean up, she realized that she was leaving with more questions than answers.

* * *

"I should have bought more sunscreen," Bess said as she, Nancy, and George stood on the long dock to watch the jump competition. "I didn't realize the sun would be so strong here."

George took in Bess's large straw hat, sunglasses, and the thick lotion she had spread over every exposed part of her body. "You'd have to be in a tent to be better covered," George said dryly.

Bess glanced back at the tournament tent. "That's not a bad idea."

Nancy laughed. She looked out at the lake, where a large wedge-shaped jumping ramp had been set up in the water. They had already watched several skiers make the fast glide up the ramp and then fly more than a hundred feet above the water. The competition was heated, and the crowd grew more excited with each jump.

George nudged Nancy. "I think Katie's next," she said, pointing to a skier gathering speed in the approach to the ramp. Nancy nodded. She had her binoculars up to her eyes.

Katie was going so fast that she seemed to skim above the water. She pulled both skis to one side of the wake, readying herself for the jump. Then she slid up onto the ramp, exploding off the top edge.

Nancy watched breathlessly as Katie flew through the air, still hanging on to the tow rope.

Shouts of awe and surprise came from the people on the dock as Katie hung suspended in midair. When she finally landed on the water again, the spectators burst into applause.

"Wow!" Nancy exclaimed. "That had to be the best jump yet."

"Did you see how high she was?" George said.

The crowd quieted to hear the announcer state Katie's jump length over the loudspeaker. The scratchy electronic voice could be heard up and down the beach. "One hundred forty-five feet for Katie Cobb."

The crowd erupted into cheers again. Katie's jump was nearly twenty feet longer than Pam Cartwright's, who was now in second place.

"If she can do that on the first jump, imagine what she'll do on the next two!" Bess said excitedly.

"I doubt she'll even take her next two," George said. "That jump will easily put her in the top half of the competitors, so she'll definitely compete in tomorrow's round. She's allowed to skip her other turns today—that way she can save her energy."

"Let's go congratulate her," Nancy suggested. The three girls walked back to the landing area.

Suddenly they heard shouts from that end of the beach. Nancy took off her sunglasses and saw a small group of people standing at the water's edge in the landing area. They were waving their fists and chanting in unison, "Out of the lake! Out of the lake!"

"What's going on?" Bess asked.

"I bet that's the Blue Waters group," George said.

"Blue Waters?" Nancy repeated.

"It's an environmental group that's trying to stop development around the lake," George explained. "They're against commercial uses of the lake, such as this tournament. I saw one of their fliers when I was in the tournament tent this morning."

Nancy, Bess, and George came within twenty feet of the landing area. As Katie's boat spun around to drop her off near the beach, the protesters moved over to stand in front of her.

Stepping out of her skis in the shallow water, Katie seemed surprised to see a group of people shaking their fists at her. She picked her skis up and waded to shore.

Four people broke away from the Blue Waters group and blocked her path. A tall man with a reddish brown beard began yelling at Katie, gesturing toward the lake and then pointing back at her.

Nancy finally reached the edge of the group, and Katie caught sight of her. "Excuse me," Katie said to the tall man. "I really need to go dry off."

She stepped back into the water to go around him. Nancy cut through the group to meet her.

As Katie waded past the man, he suddenly leapt into the shallow water toward her. Grabbing hold of one of the skis she was holding, he yanked it from her hand. As Katie fell backward Nancy saw her expression of terror.

The man had lifted the ski into the air and was starting to bring it down on Katie's head!

5

Still Waters Run Deep

Nancy made a running leap for the bearded man. As he was lowering the ski, Nancy grabbed his right arm with both hands. Yanking hard, she made him lose his grip on the ski and it dropped into the water with a harmless splash.

The man jerked away from Nancy, almost falling into the shallow water. "Careful!" another protester yelled, helping the bearded man remain upright. The small knot of demonstrators had stopped chanting and started to surround Nancy. Bess and George hurried over to stand with their friend.

The bearded man whirled around to Nancy, and she felt her muscles tense. "What do you think you're doing?" he spat out. "How dare you attack me!" His deceptively soft voice was full of anger.

Nancy drew herself up, feeling a little angry herself. "Attack you?" she said evenly. "I was trying to stop you from hurting my friend."

The man took a menacing step toward Nancy. "It's your friend who's hurting the lake and our other natural resources."

"She's not hurting anything," Bess blurted out.

"What?" he exclaimed, his eyes flashing at Bess. "Are you all that ignorant? This whole tournament is a complete misuse of the lake." The protesters around him began to nod and murmur, "Yeah! Tell her, Miller!"

Nancy heard more voices behind her, and she turned to see Mr. and Mrs. Cobb, Jackie Albert, and the tournament director break their way through the circle of people.

"Everything okay here, honey?" Mr. Cobb asked, handing Katie a towel. He wedged himself between Katie and Miller, glaring at Miller. Katie nodded and wrapped the towel around herself.

Just then the tournament director, whose name badge read Pat McKiernan, stepped in front of the protest leader. "Miller, you know the rules," he said, sounding more than a bit exasperated. "Stay away from the skiers and the ski areas. We've got more skiers coming in."

"And that's just the trouble!" Miller retorted. "You won't stop until you've ruined the entire lake."

Pat McKiernan took a deep breath. "I don't

41

want to have to call the authorities," he said, obviously trying to stay calm, "but I will."

Miller threw his hands up. "All right, all right," he said. "But don't think you won't be seeing us later." He and the rest of the Blue Waters group trooped back off up the beach.

Pat McKiernan turned to Nancy, Katie, and the others. "I'm sorry," he apologized. "They have a right to demonstrate, but they were told to stay a hundred yards away from any skier." Although he was dressed in shorts and a T-shirt, McKiernan had the crisp, organized manner of a business executive. Curly red hair poked out from under his baseball cap.

"Who is Miller?" Nancy asked.

"Miller Burton is the leader of the Blue Waters organization," McKiernan replied. "Their goal is to prevent overdevelopment of the lake area. Apparently they feel that the tournament brings too much traffic and pollution to the area, and the speedboats deplete the lake of its water. I sympathize with them and their goals, but Miller can be such an extremist that it's hard to support him." McKiernan shook his head.

"Anyway, back to the tournament," he said, shrugging at Katie. "Congratulations on a terrific jump, Katie—it looks like we'll have a great round tomorrow." McKiernan clapped Katie on the shoulder and then headed back to the tournament tent.

"The jump!" Bess exclaimed. "I almost forgot. Katie, it was amazing!"

The wide grin returned to Katie's face. "Thanks. It *felt* pretty amazing—everything just clicked. Mom, what you said about positioning my legs at the takeoff really helped."

Mrs. Cobb smiled. "Good," she said.

As the group headed for the Cobbs' umbrella, Nancy, Katie, and Jackie fell behind, walking slowly up the beach. Nancy was deep in thought.

"It's a shame that such a good jump had to end with that demonstration," Jackie said. "I hope it didn't throw you off."

Katie laughed shakily. "Well, I am beginning to feel as though I have a bull's-eye painted on me," she admitted.

"Katie, that might be a real possibility," Nancy said quietly.

Katie tilted her head in surprise. "What—you mean that I am a target?" she asked. "Why would anyone target me?"

Nancy shrugged and simply said, "I don't know. I don't even know that you *are* a target. I just thought I might check around a bit. And you should keep your eyes open, just in case you are in danger."

Katie turned to Jackie. "Back in River Heights Nancy is an amateur detective," she explained proudly. "But she's as good as any pro."

"Really?" Jackie said, interested. "I've always

43

loved detective stories. If you were investigating, who would be your prime suspects?"

"Well, I'd like to know more about Miller Burton," Nancy began.

"You know, I just read his name in the local paper," Jackie said slowly, scrunching up her forehead in thought. "What was it . . . Oh, yes, he was accused of shoplifting from a ski store in Truckee. It's a little town not far from here."

Nancy raised an eyebrow. "It would take you only forty-five minutes to get to Truckee," Jackie added.

"It's a cute little town," Katie put in. "They have an old-fashioned main street with lots of little shops. It might be fun."

Nancy called up to Bess and George. "How about an afternoon trip to Truckee?" she asked.

"I heard it has lots of little shops," Bess said, "so you can count me in."

George groaned at the idea of shopping, but agreed to go, too.

"Are you girls making plans?" Mrs. Cobb said as they reached the umbrella. "Don't forget that the tournament sponsors are hosting a big spaghetti dinner in Tahoe City tonight. I'd love for you all to join us."

"We wouldn't miss it," Nancy said. "Thanks, Mrs. Cobb."

* * *

44

Nancy, Bess, and George stepped out of their rental car and into the midafternoon sunshine in Truckee. They'd gone straight back to their cabin, dropping off their beach gear and changing clothes before setting out. Now Nancy and George, in shorts and T-shirts, and Bess, in a sleeveless denim blouse and shorts, were strolling up and down Commercial Row, Truckee's quaint main street.

The storefronts looked as if they'd been lifted out of the Old West, though they now housed clothing shops, jewelry boutiques, and small restaurants. "Isn't it wonderful?" Nancy exclaimed.

"Well, that depends on what 'it' is," George said. "I think the mountains are spectacular. But Bess is more interested in that store behind us." Nancy turned and saw Bess with her nose pressed up against the glass.

Nancy laughed. "Bess, the ski shop I have to check out is around the corner on that cross street," she said, pointing. "Why don't you get some shopping done and we'll meet you back at this corner in half an hour?"

Bess agreed, and Nancy and George, following the directions Jackie and Katie had given them, set off for Sierra Ski.

In a few minutes they were pushing through the heavy oak door of the shop. The store was divided into two sections, one for snow skiing and one for waterskiing. All the waterskiing equipment was prominently placed in front with racks displaying wetsuits and swimsuits and one wall stacked high with water skis.

As Nancy and George stood and looked around, a sandy-haired man in jeans walked up to them. "Can I help you, ladies?" he asked.

"I was hoping to find the manager," Nancy said.

The man smiled. "You found him," he said. "I'm Mike. What can I do for you?"

Nancy introduced herself and George and described their confrontation with Miller Burton and the Blue Waters group. "I've heard that he was accused of shoplifting from your store," Nancy said. "Is that true?"

Mike shoved his hands in his pockets and sighed. "You must have seen the newspaper account," he said. "I wish those reporters would get their stories straight. Last week Miller stopped by to drop off some pamphlets. He got into a shouting match with a couple of young guys who were shopping here." He paused.

"And?" Nancy prompted him.

Mike shrugged. "That was it. The young guys made a big deal of it—they started yelling that Miller had hit them and that they saw him taking some T-shirts."

"Had he?" George asked.

Mike shook his head. "I was watching him the whole time he was here. The young men admitted later that they'd never actually seen any shoplifting."

"Do you know who those guys were?" Nancy asked.

"Never seen them before—or since," Mike said. He smiled a little. "I know Miller can be a pain, but he's really committed to his cause. I think he just gets carried away sometimes."

Nancy nodded thoughtfully. She was wondering how carried away Miller might get. As she was staring at the wall of skis, a thought hit her.

She motioned to the wall. "Most of these skis have a small fin on the bottom. I guess that helps the skier guide the ski."

Mike nodded. "Your better skiers will be concerned about the fin," he said. "The rest of us just try to stay up."

Nancy smiled. "Can the fin be adjusted?"

Mike's eyes lit up. "We sell adjustable fins," he said. "They're easy to use. You just attach one to the ski, and then you can move it to just the right position. Pro skiers might use it to control their slalom runs."

Nancy nodded slowly, thinking of Katie's fall during her slalom run that morning. But before she could ask another question, Mike continued. "In fact, I just had a coach in here asking me about adjustable fins," he said. "If you were at the tournament today, you might have seen him—Gary Trachok. He's Pam Cartwright's coach."

George coughed and glanced at Nancy. Feeling her heart jump, Nancy tried to keep her voice level as she asked, "Did he buy a fin?"

"No, he said he already had one," Mike said. "He just wanted me to demonstrate some of the new ones that allow you to make minute adjustments."

"Are they difficult to adjust?" Nancy asked.

"Oh, no," Mike said. "You could make a change on a fin while sitting on the dock."

Mike excused himself to help a customer, and Nancy and George left the shop. As they did, George grabbed Nancy's arm. "I bet Trachok was asking about that fin so he could adjust Katie's ski. I know that's what made her fall," she said excitedly.

Nancy shook her head. "We don't have any proof of that," she said. "It could just be a strange coincidence that Katie fell after Trachok asked about adjusting the fin. *Very* strange," she added pointedly.

"What do we do now?" George asked.

Nancy checked her watch. "We can shop a bit with Bess," she said, "and then head for Tahoe City. We have some serious spaghetti eating ahead of us."

A few hours later Nancy pushed away her empty plate. "I can't eat another bite," she said.

"I feel the same way," Mrs. Cobb agreed. "But this garlic bread is so good, it's hard to stop."

The tournament participants and sponsors had taken over an open, airy room in one of the beachfront restaurants in Tahoe City, a few miles around the lake. Sitting at long wooden tables with red- and white-checked tablecloths, they were enjoying spaghetti, garlic bread, and green salad.

Almost three full sides of the room were glass, which gave a wide vista of Lake Tahoe. The still waters of the lake were reflecting the fading oranges and reds of the sunset sky.

The Cobbs sat across from Nancy, Bess, and George, Bridget between her parents. The young girl glanced up occasionally to stare intently at Nancy. Some people were still eating, while others were already mingling.

"Everyone is so relaxed here," George said. "It's hard to believe you're all competing against one another."

"Oh, we're competitive when we have to be," Katie said, finishing up her salad. "But since you run into the same people from tournament to tournament, you tend to become friends."

Nancy let her eyes wander out the long window next to her. Boats bobbed in the water on either side of a short pier. She saw someone walk out onto the dock, stopping often to gaze out at the lake. As the person turned, Nancy saw that it was Pam Cartwright.

Nancy stood up and excused herself from the table, saying she'd be right back. This was a good chance to speak to Pam alone. If Katie's mishaps weren't accidents, someone had to have a reason to want Katie knocked out of the competition. Nancy knew Pam was her main rival for the overall title—and Gary Trachok was Pam's coach.

As she reached for the knob to open one of the side doors that led to the beach, Nancy was startled by a hand on her arm. She whirled around to find Trachok standing behind her.

"Where are you off to now, Ms. Drew?" he said in a quiet, sarcastic voice. "A little more spying? Have the Cobbs hired their own spy now?"

Nancy pulled her arm away from his hand. "I'm going for a walk," she said calmly. "As far as I know, the beach is open to everyone." She slipped out the door onto the darkening beach. It was easy to understand why the Cobbs felt Katie would be better off without Trachok, she thought.

Outside, the clatter of the dinner faded to be replaced by the gentle lapping of water. Nancy slipped off her shoes to walk more easily in the sand. As she approached the dock she saw another figure had joined Pam on the dock.

Nancy hurried onto the dock and, moving quietly down one side, saw that it was Jackie Albert who had joined Pam. Nancy frowned. Was Katie right—were all the competitors friends? Keeping near the boats on the right side, she crept up toward them, hoping to overhear their conversation. The dock creaked as boats bumped against it, and Nancy tried to blend her footsteps in with the creaks.

Without warning Pam and Jackie turned around to walk back to the beach. Nancy stopped dead. She peered around for a place to hide, her heart beating rapidly. She didn't want to be caught spying on them.

As the two came closer, Nancy quickly slipped down into the sailboat nearest her, crouching low against the side. She backed up against a pile of damp canvas tarps.

Slowly she brought her head up, watching the dock. As Jackie and Pam approached the sailboat, she heard the low murmur of their voices, but none of the words was distinct. They paused for a moment in midstride, then turned and headed back out toward the end of the dock.

Nancy sighed. It would be difficult to catch their conversation now, but she might be able to hear the tail end. She began to rise from the boat

51

when she heard a loud creak behind her. She froze. The sound had definitely come from inside the boat.

Turning her head slightly, Nancy saw something move behind the canvas tarps. Her heart leapt into her throat. Someone was inside the sailboat with her!

Nancy sprang up. A sudden reflection on the water caught her eye and she jerked around.

Something cold and hard banged against her head, throwing her off balance. In the next instant Nancy was pitching sideways over the gunwale into the inky water!

6

Someone Is Watching

With a loud splash Nancy plunged into the icy lake. Completely submerged, she thrashed about, struggling to orient herself. Following the line of bubbles upward, she made her way to the surface. Finally she pulled her head out and thirstily gulped lungfuls of air.

Nancy circled her arms and legs, treading water. She tossed her wet hair out of her face and wiped the water from her eyes. The sudden movement caused an intense throbbing in her head.

The sailboat she had tumbled from was rocking back and forth from the impact of her fall. The boat appeared to be empty now—her brief seconds underwater must have given her attacker time to escape.

She heard the sound of running on the wooden dock. Jackie Albert and Pam Cartwright were peering down at her, visible in the faint glow from the restaurant lights.

"Nancy!" Jackie cried in surprise. Nancy paddled to the dock, and the two girls helped her up. "What hap—" Jackie began.

"Did you see anyone running off the dock?" Nancy gasped.

"No." The girls shook their heads, perplexed.

"I'll be right back," Nancy said, taking off toward the beach. She could hear Jackie call for her to wait, but she didn't want to waste time explaining. Whoever had been in the boat with her already had a head start.

Nancy ran down the dock, scanning the boats and the water between them. When she reached the beach she stopped, searching up and down the stretch of sand. Except for a couple strolling along the shore about a hundred yards away, the beach was deserted.

Peering up at the restaurant Nancy could see that the room was still filled with people eating and talking. She shivered in frustration and turned around. Rubbing the tender spot on her head, she could feel the bruise that was already forming.

Jackie and Pam caught up with her. "Sorry to take off like that," Nancy said to them. "I thought

I could catch the person who knocked me into the water."

Jackie and Pam seemed startled by her statement. "Uh, Nancy, this is Pam Cartwright," Jackie said hurriedly. "Pam, this is Nancy Drew, a friend of Katie. So, Nancy, tell us what happened."

Nancy described the incident to Jackie and Pam, leaving out the real reason she had been in the boat. Instead she told the skiers she had been strolling on the dock, looking at the boats. Picking out the sailboat she had been hiding in, Nancy saw that its boom—the large horizontal bar that held the bottom of the sail—was swinging around loosely with the rocking motion of the boat. She realized that the boom could have hit her.

"Did you see or hear anyone on the dock?" Nancy asked the skiers again.

Both Jackie and Pam shook their heads. "But we were talking, so I really wasn't paying attention," Pam admitted. "Were you able to get a look at the person in the boat?"

"I didn't see the face," Nancy said. "But I'm pretty sure it was a man. His shoulders were fairly broad." She shivered and realized that her cold, wet clothes were sticking to her skin.

"Let's get you back to the restaurant so you can dry off," Pam offered.

As they reached the door to the restaurant,

Jackie pulled Nancy aside. "You wait here while I get Bess and George," she said. Then, as Pam went inside, Jackie whispered to Nancy, "I wouldn't be surprised if Gary Trachok was behind this. Once he sees you know Katie, you'll be an enemy of his." Then Jackie slipped through the door.

Dripping wet, Nancy stood on the narrow bark-chip pathway, staring after them. If Trachok *was* behind this, Nancy reflected, Pam didn't seem to be working with him—she acted surprised by the whole incident.

A few minutes later Bess and George came hurrying outside. When they caught sight of Nancy their mouths dropped open in surprise.

"What happened to you?" Bess asked, handing her friend her sweater.

"A little unexpected swim," Nancy said. She led the way to the parking lot. "I was watching Jackie and Pam from a boat moored to the dock when I noticed there was someone in the boat with me. The next thing I knew, something knocked me on the head and I fell in the water."

They reached the car, and George slid into the driver's seat. Bess found a beach towel in the backseat and gave it to Nancy, who rubbed her hair before settling into the passenger seat.

"So you didn't really get to see who was in the boat with you?" George asked as she drove back to Incline Village.

"No," Nancy said. "But I do think it was a man. Jackie might be right about Gary Trachok—he saw me going outside and accused me of spying."

"But why would Trachok knock you in the head?" Bess asked. "I thought it was Katie who was being targeted."

"Well, if someone is after Katie, this might be a warning for me to keep my nose out of it," Nancy considered. "Or maybe someone is trying to sabotage the entire tournament and Katie is only the first victim. Or maybe the person in the boat was unrelated to the tournament and was just sleeping there. The only thing I'm sure of is that it wasn't Pam or Jackie. They're the only people whose whereabouts I know for certain."

"Good morning!" Bess called cheerfully as Nancy entered the kitchen the next morning. Sunlight streamed in through the large windows, warming the sharp, cool air in the cabin. Already Nancy could hear birds singing outside, and she could smell the buttermilk pancakes Bess was flipping on a skillet.

"Mmmm," Nancy murmured, watching Bess add some pancakes to a pile on a plate. "I'm surprised George hasn't smelled these yet," she said.

"George is out for a run," Bess said, bringing the plate over to a round wooden table.

"Well, if she doesn't get back soon, there might

not be any left," Nancy said, helping herself to the pancakes.

"How's your head?" Bess asked, joining Nancy at the table.

Nancy pulled her reddish blond hair back to reveal a small lump. "It only hurts when I touch it," she said. As she was pouring syrup on her pancakes, a knock came on the front door. "I guess George forgot her key," Nancy said, crossing through the living room. She opened the door.

"Katie!" she exclaimed. Katie Cobb stood in the doorway, wearing shorts and a hooded sweatshirt.

"Hi," Katie said. "Sorry we missed you last night—we left the restaurant before you got back from your walk on the beach."

"Come in and have some pancakes," Nancy said. Noticing that Katie looked a bit down, Nancy decided to wait a few minutes before explaining the events of the night before to her.

Nancy led her friend into the kitchen. "Hi!" Bess said. "I thought you'd already be at the beach."

Katie leaned against the counter, her hands in her pockets. "The first round this morning is jump, and my jump from yesterday has given me a big lead," she explained. "Mom and I talked and we decided to skip this round. I should still make it into the finals tomorrow, but this way I won't risk getting injured or tired out."

"Can you do that with your other events, too?" Bess asked.

Katie shook her head. "No. My longest jump can count for the whole tournament, but the trick and slalom scores don't carry over from the previous day."

Nancy studied her friend carefully. "Is anything wrong, Katie?" she asked.

Katie sighed. "Sort of," she said. "I think someone tried to break into my bedroom last night."

"What?" Bess exclaimed.

Katie slowly began to explain. "I woke up in the middle of the night to hear a scraping sound—as if the window sash was being pulled up. I got up to check and saw a shadow at the window." She paused for a second. "I got a little scared and called out, 'Who's there?' Then I saw the window drop back down, and the shadow disappeared.

"I woke my dad and asked him to check outside the cabin," Katie went on. "He couldn't find anything. I didn't sleep too well the rest of the night, but I don't think the person came back."

"You poor thing." Bess sighed.

Katie smiled weakly. "I have to admit, I'm

59

getting a little spooked," she said in a strained voice. "I mean, is someone really after me? Is that what the problems yesterday were about?" she asked Nancy.

Nancy hesitated for a moment. "That's what I'm beginning to think," she said quietly. Then she told Katie about the pin in the release rope mechanism. "I'm afraid you're in danger."

Katie looked shocked and then pained. "But who would do that?" she asked. "Could somebody really hate me that much?"

"I don't know," Nancy said. "Your two accidents could have been coincidences, I suppose. But I had an accident myself last night outside the restaurant in Tahoe City. Someone knocked me into the water."

Katie's face went white. "Who?" she gasped.

"I couldn't see his face," Nancy said. "But you told me yesterday that Gary Trachok was still angry at you and your parents for being fired— do you think he might be out for revenge?"

Katie drew back in surprise and then shook her head. "I know better than anyone that Gary can be a jerk," she said. "But I don't think he'd ever hurt anyone. Besides a stunt like jamming the release mechanism could get him—and Pam— thrown off the tour. I don't think he'd take that risk."

Then Nancy told Katie that Gary had been

60

asking about adjustable ski fins in Truckee. Katie's eyes grew wide, and she sank down into a chair.

"As it happens, I checked my ski last night," she admitted slowly. "My fin *was* moved."

Nancy sat back down at the table, considering the evidence. Gary was obviously bitter toward the Cobbs. He had been asking about adjustable ski fins and was clearly interested in Nancy's investigation of the release rope. Still she didn't want to jump to a hasty conclusion.

Nancy watched Katie's face, wondering if she should ask her next question. She chose her words carefully and said, "Katie, I don't want to pry, but I couldn't help noticing that Bridget seems a little . . . withdrawn."

Katie's face immediately flushed. "I know," she said softly. "Bridget's been in a bad mood, to say the least. I think she's angry at me, but I don't know why. She was so rude to Mom last night, Mom almost grounded her for the rest of the tournament."

Katie dropped her eyes to the table. "Bridget used to be into skiing when we moved to California. Now she can't even stand to talk about it."

Nancy glanced at Bess. She wanted to know more about Bridget's moodiness, but the subject obviously upset Katie.

"Well," Nancy said, standing up, "we're not

61

going to solve this case by sitting here. Katie, do you mind if I look around your cabin before you go to the beach?''

Bess piped up, "I'll wait here for George—and help her finish these pancakes."

The Cobbs' cabin was about half a mile from the one Nancy and her friends were renting. The small streets between the cabins were empty with only an occasional jogger or dog walker passing. The dense forest came right to the side of the road, blanketing the area in quiet. Katie seemed lost in her own thoughts so Nancy didn't disturb her.

"Everyone was still asleep when I left," Katie whispered when they approached her cabin.

Nancy nodded and circled the small A-frame. There were sliding glass doors in front. On the ground level a redwood deck without rails surrounded three sides of the cabin. Katie pointed out her bedroom window on the right side of the cabin.

The cabin was the last one on the street, so the right side was bordered only by woods, stretching as far as Nancy could see. Tall evergreens and smaller bushes came up to the edge of the deck on that side.

Nancy looked around the deck just beneath Katie's small window. Except for a few pine needles and ants, the deck was clean.

She stepped off the deck onto the ground,

letting her eyes roam around the underbrush. Bending down, she noticed that the space between the deck and the ground hadn't been filled in, leaving a crawlspace about a foot high.

Nancy lay flat on the ground, peering into the space under the deck. It was hard to see, so Nancy thrust her hand in, sifting through the debris. Her hand ran across leaves, rocks, dirt, and a few tiny pine cones. Sweeping her arm over them a couple of times, she dragged it all out into the sunlight.

Kneeling, Nancy poked through the little pile with Katie peering over her shoulder. Her eyes were immediately drawn to something white in the dark-colored pile.

Grabbing it with her thumb and index finger, Nancy pulled out a piece of paper. She could tell it couldn't have been under the deck long—the paper was too clean and dry, still bright white.

Katie leaned in closer, staring at the paper with wide eyes. In the quiet morning air Nancy could hear Katie's soft breathing next to her ear. Nancy shook the dirt from the paper and brought it up to eye level.

A sharp crack behind them suddenly broke the silence. Nancy whirled around, searching through the trees.

A figure in white darted out from behind a tree and headed into the woods. Someone had been observing them!

7

Target: Katie Cobb

Nancy realized that the person was trying to get away. Jumping up, she watched as the flash of white wove through the trees.

With the paper still in hand, Nancy ran after the white figure, darting around the evergreens. The ground was uneven, covered with sticks and rocks, and Nancy stumbled over a half-buried root, but remained upright.

The trees gave way to a line of green, leafy bushes, some as tall as Nancy. As the bushes swayed and rustled several yards ahead, Nancy could follow the path of the person she was chasing. She pushed her way into the bushes and saw that they lined the bank of a small creek. She reasoned that the figure was running beside the creek.

Soon she was enveloped in the thick growth,

straining to hear. She stopped and stood perfectly still. The crackling and rustling up ahead had stopped, too.

Nancy tried to control her breathing so she could listen more carefully. The only sound was the chattering of a chipmunk. Had she lost the person?

It was impossible to see ahead through all the bushes. Nancy took off for a clearing to her left where shafts of early morning sunlight fell through the trees. Surrounded again by evergreens Nancy looked at the top of the line of bushes, hoping to glimpse any movement. As she walked along she squinted through the alternating patches of sunlight and shade.

Finally Nancy stopped. Whoever had been spying on them had used the cover of the forest well. The person might be crouched in a bush right next to her or could be running a quarter of a mile ahead. Nancy couldn't comb the entire area that quickly.

She turned back toward the cabin, wondering who it had been. No one except Bess had known that she and Katie would be at the Cobbs', so no one could have planned a stakeout. But if the person had merely been a stranger out for a walk, he or she wouldn't have taken off like that.

Was it the same person who had tried to break into the cabin the night before? she wondered. Perhaps the person was trying to collect something he or she had dropped—something like a piece of paper.

"Thank goodness you're all right," Katie said when Nancy emerged from the woods. "I lost you after a couple of minutes. Did you see anyone?"

Nancy shook her head. "Just a flash of white," she said. "Whoever it was knew how to get through the woods in a hurry."

"Do you think the person was really watching us?" Katie asked. "And—was it the same person who was trying to get into our cabin last night?" She sounded as if she didn't want to believe that.

Instead of answering Nancy held up the paper in her hand. Katie stood next to her to take a look. Smoothing it out, Nancy saw that it was actually the torn quarter of a sheet of white bond paper. In the upper left-hand corner was an official logo: a small drawing of a lake and the words *Blue Waters* printed in block letters with an Incline Village address.

On the paper was a neatly typed line: "Katie, don't press your luck—get out now!"

Nancy and Katie read the note quickly. The skier shook her head and frowned when she caught Nancy's eye.

"Well, I guess that settles that," Katie said, trying to sound brave. "I guess I really am a bull's-eye." Her voice cracked as she spoke the last word.

"Don't worry," Nancy said, putting an arm

around Katie. "I'll do my best to find out who's doing this and put a stop to it."

Katie appeared to be surprised. "It's got to be what's-his-name and those Blue Waters people, doesn't it?" she said. "The note is on their stationery."

"It *looks* like it was Miller Burton," Nancy admitted. "In fact, it's a perfect clue—too perfect, really. If Miller is the one who's after you, why would he be so obvious as to use his own stationery? It makes no sense."

Katie glanced at the cabin and sighed. "I'd better go inside," she said. "I'm sure my parents are awake by now, and I don't want them to worry."

"I think you have to tell them what's been going on," Nancy urged.

Katie nodded. "I will. See you at the beach."

Nancy headed back to her cabin, folding the warning note into the pocket of her sweatshirt and thinking about Miller Burton.

The environmental protester had made it clear that he was opposed to the tournament, and since Katie was a top contender, targeting her made sense. Miller had been at the beach the day before, and he probably could have gained access to Katie's ski and the release rope.

The note in her pocket bothered her, though. If Miller *had* been the one behind the skiing sabotage, then he had been doing it anonymously. So why would he suddenly give away his identity through the note? Nancy wondered.

If it wasn't him, who had access to his stationery?

By the time Nancy entered her cabin her mind was racing with questions. She was afraid that if she didn't answer them soon, Katie could be in real danger.

About an hour later Nancy, Bess, and George were standing at the top of the Sand Harbor launch area, scanning the beach. It was already filled with groups of people in beach chairs with coolers, and colorful towels. Looking out to the water, Nancy saw that the jump ramp was already being towed in. She realized that that day's jump competition must be already over.

George nudged her. "I think that's Mr. Cobb waving at us down there," she said, pointing.

Nancy saw Katie's father standing by the Cobbs' umbrella. She waved back, and he motioned for the three of them to join them.

"How did the jump round go?" Nancy asked when they reached the umbrella. Mr. and Mrs. Cobb, Katie, and Bridget were sitting quietly in their beach chairs.

"Oh, fine," Mr. Cobb said distractedly. "No one today scored a jump as long as Katie's jump yesterday." Nancy noticed that despite the good news his face was gray and drawn.

"Great!" Bess said brightly. "So what's next—slalom?"

Mrs. Cobb stood up, a worried expression on her face. "Maybe what's next is pulling out of the tournament," she blurted out. "Katie just told us about the pin in the release rope and Nancy's mishap in the sailboat. With the attempted break-in last night . . ." She threw up her hands. "Maybe we're just inviting trouble by staying here."

"Mom, I told you that Nancy is investigating it," Katie said from her chair. "Besides, dropping out is just what this person wants me to do." She shook her head determinedly. "I'm not going to give whoever it is that satisfaction."

Mr. Cobb nodded slowly. "She does have a point," he said to his wife.

Mrs. Cobb took a deep breath and searched Nancy's face. "Nancy, you know I trust your skills, but surely you can understand my concern. What if this person gets to Katie before you find out who it is?"

"I do understand your concern, Mrs. Cobb," Nancy said calmly. "And to be honest, I can't give you a guarantee. I can only promise to do my best."

Mrs. Cobb crossed her arms and settled her mouth into a thin, tight line. She silently bent her head, obviously thinking hard.

Katie's voice piped up behind her. "I've got a

shot at winning," she said quietly. "And it's my first time competing for the overall title."

Mrs. Cobb turned to face her daughter. Their eyes met for a long moment. "Okay," Mrs. Cobb said finally. "We'll stay with it." She whirled around to face Nancy. "And I hope you'll stay with it, too."

"Oh, she will," Bess said before Nancy could respond. "Nancy never gives up on a case."

"She'd better not," Bridget said sourly. Nancy turned to look at her. The younger girl sat slouched low in her beach chair, playing with the fringe on her cut-off denim shorts. "I mean, the tournament's not even half over. A lot could still happen," she said. She raised her head and stared straight at Nancy with a look of defiance.

"Thanks for your optimism, Bridg," Katie said dryly.

Standing up, Katie squinted at the tournament tent, then pulled off her T-shirt and put on a life vest over her red swimsuit. "They're about to announce the start of the slalom," she said. Turning to Bridget, she asked, "How about riding in the boat during my run? I could use some advice along the way."

"No, thanks. I need to rest," she said. Grabbing a towel, she got up and wandered off to a spot in the sand away from the umbrella.

Katie shrugged at her parents. "I tried," she said, picking up her black slalom ski.

Mr. Cobb nodded. "I'll talk to her," he said. "Go make it a good run."

As Katie turned toward the shore, Mrs. Cobb grabbed her arm. "Now, don't forget—that first turn is crucial. Get ready for it early and extend yourself fully. That rope is shorter and is going to feel shorter still."

Katie nodded, her face a serious study of concentration. George is right, Nancy thought. Katie did seem to be able to focus her energy, despite the earlier mishaps and worries.

With a final smile of encouragement Mrs. Cobb, followed by Bess and George, headed for a good vantage point on the shore. Nancy walked with Katie to the water's edge.

The same man who'd driven the boat for Katie the day before was backing the boat away from the shore. Wading into the lake, Katie dropped her ski on the water's surface. She stepped out farther and splashed some water on her arms. Then she rolled her shoulders around, trying to stay loose and relaxed.

After slipping off her sandals, Nancy waded out to fetch the floating ski. She grabbed it by the black, rubbery front boot, the part that held the skier's front foot snugly in the ski. Pulling the ski toward her, she frowned.

She yanked on the boot again, and as she did, her heart sank. Lifting the ski from the water, Nancy turned to Katie.

71

Squinting, Katie held out her hand to receive the ski. "Wait a minute," Nancy said grimly.

Silently Nancy showed her friend the ski boot. Katie's mouth dropped open. "Oh, no!" she cried. "My boot's ripped. It looks as if it's been slashed!"

8

Danger at the Water's Edge

Katie grabbed the ski from Nancy. She pulled the front boot apart as if she were going to slip it on. As she did, her hand moved through a long gash.

Katie dropped the ski in the water. "I don't believe it," she said. "How could this have happened? I just used this ski yesterday—it wasn't ripped then."

Nancy wrinkled her forehead as she concentrated. She had been thinking the same thing. The ski had been locked in the Cobbs' cabin overnight. At the beach Katie kept the ski with her other belongings under the umbrella. Whoever slashed the boot must have done it that morning on the beach while none of the Cobbs was watching.

Unless it was one of the Cobbs who had done it.

Bridget! With a sinking feeling Nancy realized that she couldn't ignore that possibility any longer.

"Hey!" a man's voice called. Nancy saw that the driver of the boat had circled back near the shore. "You ready?"

Katie held up her hand to the driver to indicate that she needed five more minutes. Then she scanned the shore lined with spectators, and spotted Pat McKiernan standing near the judge stand. She waved to him, and he walked over to meet her a few yards up the beach.

Katie held up the ski to show it to Mr. McKiernan. "I need five minutes to get another ski," she said. He looked at the damaged boot and nodded. Then he went back to tell the judges that there would be a short delay.

Nancy had been admiring Katie's cool professionalism, but now, as Katie turned back to her, Nancy saw the first signs of panic on her friend's face. "Oh, Nancy, this is my favorite ski," she began, struggling to keep her voice calm. "I'm not superstitious or anything, but I use this ski for every tournament slalom run—I just ski better on it. Now it's ruined—what am I going to do?"

"You do have other skis?" Nancy asked.

"Sure," Katie said. "But this is the one I've been practicing on. I'm used to the feel of it." She sounded ready to give up.

"Listen," Nancy said. "You don't have time to

worry about it. Just keep focusing on the course and tell me where I can find another ski for you."

"There's one in the back of our car. The car keys should be in Mom's straw beach bag," Katie said numbly.

Nancy ran up the beach to the Cobb's umbrella. She saw Mr. and Mrs. Cobb standing at the water's edge, preparing to film Katie's slalom run. Bridget was standing behind them, staring at the mountains in the distance. She dug the car keys out of Mrs. Cobb's bag, then trotted up to the parking lot. She quickly found the Cobbs' car, a red four-wheel-drive wagon big enough to cart around lots of ski equipment.

Opening the back door of the wagon, Nancy located another slalom ski. Cautiously she checked the two black rubber boots on the ski to make sure they hadn't been damaged. Then she locked the car and was back down at the shore in two minutes.

When she reached the water's edge, Nancy saw that Jackie Albert had run over and had her arm around Katie.

"You're all set," Nancy said to Katie, trying to sound confident.

"Thanks, Nancy." Katie smiled brightly.

"Just remember," Jackie reminded Katie, "it's not the ski that matters, it's the skier. Just concentrate on the first turn."

Katie took some deep breaths and Nancy saw

her concentration slowly return. She waved to the driver, waded into the water, and pulled the ski on.

A minute later the tow rope was tossed out to Katie. She grabbed it, hopping on one foot along the lake bottom. Then, sitting in the water, she pulled her other foot into the back boot, specially made for the slalom ski. The driver inched the boat forward and Katie nodded.

The boat took off with a loud roar, and the rope unfurled, yanking Katie forward. Nancy watched her settle in behind the boat as it headed toward the slalom course.

Nancy picked up the first ski and closely inspected the damaged front boot. A slit had been made from the top of the back flap to the bottom. A thin line ran slightly diagonally, from left to right, almost undetectable. The incision looked as if it had been made with a very sharp knife.

"Nancy, is everything all right?"

Nancy raised her eyes from the ski. Mrs. Cobb was hurrying up to her, saying, "There was a delay, and then I thought I saw you go get Katie's other ski—"

Nancy pulled down the flap of the ski boot to show Katie's mom the cut. Mrs. Cobb's shoulders drooped and she shook her head. "Oh, no," she whispered.

"But you know Katie," Jackie quickly put in. "She bounced right back." She pointed to the slalom course, where Katie had begun her run. A cheer went up from the crowd gathered along the shoreline.

Nancy watched as Katie swung out hard to the right, approaching the first buoy. A shorter rope was used for this round, making it more difficult for the skier to move around each buoy.

With her arms outstretched, Katie leaned to the left, pushing the ski to her right. Using her arms and body as if they were extensions of the rope, Katie leaned over the first buoy. From the shore she appeared to be almost horizontal as her ski cut neatly around the orange marker. Katie eased back into a vertical position as she headed for the second buoy.

Suddenly Nancy felt something brush against her shoulder. Then she was shoved to the side. Stepping out to catch herself, she turned to see a short woman in jeans and a Blue Waters T-shirt plant herself firmly in front of Nancy. Her right arm was linked through the arm of a young man next to her.

Nancy scanned the length of the shore and saw that a human chain was forming, forcing the skiing spectators back. Several surprised spectators near Nancy cried out, "Hey!" or "What——?" as they were pushed aside.

Then a voice suddenly blared through a bullhorn, filling the air with its staticky sound. "These waters are officially closed!"

Nancy turned to see Miller Burton with an electronic megaphone to his mouth. A group of protesters were clustered around him, holding a large banner that read Save the Lake Now!

The fifty other protesters were preventing anyone from entering or leaving the water.

Nancy strained to see over the heads of the people linking arms. It was impossible for her to watch the rest of Katie's slalom run. But when she finally spotted Katie again on the lake, the skier was cutting expertly around the sixth buoy.

Katie straightened up and punched her fist into the air. Nancy grinned, relieved. Katie must have made her run perfectly.

Just then Miller Burton's amplified voice came over the bullhorn again. "Until everyone learns to respect this resource, no one will be allowed to use it!" he said loudly, emphasizing each word.

Some spectators began to boo. A few people tried to push their way through the human chain. The protesters held their ground, though, shoving back. "No way!" one protester, a middle-aged woman, yelled.

Nancy saw the director, Pat McKiernan, walking toward Burton. McKiernan's face was set.

Carrying the broken ski with her, Nancy headed down to the beach to join Bess and George. Jackie tagged along behind her.

As the two young women reached the landing

area, the center of tournament activity, Nancy saw that Burton's protest was causing quite a disruption. Pam Cartwright, who was supposed to ski next in the slalom event, was trying to get into the water as was her driver. But the protesters continued to push them back.

Some angry spectators were trying to batter an opening through the human chain of protesters. Nancy spotted Gary Trachok among them. The Save Tahoe people wouldn't budge, though, and tempers were beginning to flare.

Feeling uneasy, Nancy skirted the landing area and found Bess and George in a group on the far side, watching the struggle.

"I don't think the protesters will let Katie get out of the water," George said, pointing to the lake. Nancy saw that Katie was looking for a place to land.

Nancy showed George and Bess the slashed ski. "It looks like someone didn't want her to get in, either," Nancy replied grimly.

The three girls turned back toward the landing area as a flurry of loud voices drew near. Nancy saw that two sheriff's deputies had appeared on the beach. Along with Pat McKiernan the deputies were trying to separate the angry knot of spectators from the protesters.

Burton continued to yell into his bullhorn. "You hypocrites call yourselves lovers of the outdoors," he shouted. "But here we are, in the middle of a drought, and you're pulling precious water out of the lake with these speedboats!"

As one of the deputies took hold of Burton's arm, he squirmed away, twisting back toward the shore. At the same time Katie had been dropped off by the boat and was coasting into shore. Ski in hand, she hit the shallow water right in front of Miller Burton and the Blue Waters group who had rallied around their banner.

Nancy saw Katie trying to figure out what was going on. Suddenly Burton broke through two of his protesters and splashed into the shallow water. He thrust his bullhorn right into Katie's face.

"Here she is!" he yelled. "Katie Cobb, the biggest hypocrite of all. She calls herself an athlete, but she's really a money-hungry, self-promoting nature killer. Don't be fooled!"

Katie was obviously shocked, and she flinched back from the high-volume squeal of the bullhorn. The deputies grabbed Burton's arms to pull him back.

Before they could, though, he leaned toward Katie, his face red and his eyes narrowed into steely slits. "Just you wait," he snarled hoarsely. "Soon—very soon—the tables will be turned on you, Ms. Cobb!"

9

The Donner Party

The sheriff's deputies pulled a fierce Miller Burton away from Katie.

Nancy peeked over the human chain to observe Katie. Her mouth had dropped open, and her eyes were flashing. This latest outburst against her seemed to be the last straw.

"Number one, you don't own this lake," Katie snapped back at Burton. The crowd suddenly fell silent as everyone listened to Katie's response. "And number two, the skiers and boaters have helped your cause, not hurt it," she went on. "Nobody is more careful than we are about following boating rules and limiting our use of the lake. That's more than I can say for *your* group. You don't follow any rules!"

A few of the spectators began clapping in support of Katie. As she noticed the crowd watching her, her face turned crimson. Still angry, she marched out of the water with careful splashes, leaving Burton behind in her wake.

Nancy saw Mrs. Cobb hurry over to the edge of the sand where Katie was now standing. Taking the ski out of her daughter's hand, she said quietly, "Come on. You'll get cold standing here."

Meanwhile, the deputies were leading Burton away. Katie's spunky response seemed to have sobered him a bit. The protesters were breaking up, and the group holding the banner moved up the beach, still chanting, "Save the lake now!"

"That guy can't say anything he wants to me," Nancy heard Katie exclaim to her mother. "I'm not a nature killer, and I'm sick of being made to feel like the enemy."

"I agree," Mrs. Cobb said. "But a confrontation here will only aggravate these people. Besides, you just had a terrific run. Don't let Miller Burton ruin that."

Mrs. Cobb led Katie over to where Nancy, Bess, George, and Jackie were standing on shore.

Just then Mr. Cobb ran up to the group. "Honey, are you all right?" he asked Katie. She nodded, and her father scowled. "These environmental terrorists were blocking my way. At least you got in a good slalom run before they barged in."

"Good?" Bess cut in. She smiled at Katie. "It

was great. I was sure you were going to fall when you were leaning over those buoys. But you timed it all perfectly."

Nancy and George looked at Bess in surprise. "Bess Marvin, waterskiing buff?" George said in disbelief.

Bess tossed her head. "You never know," she said mysteriously.

George shook her head with a smile.

"Well, I'm sure glad you're okay," Jackie said to Katie. "I need to get something to eat before trick starts. Take it easy, okay?" she said, turning from the group with a sketchy wave.

"Thanks, Jackie," Katie said.

Nancy, Bess, and George joined Mr. and Mrs. Cobb and Katie as they headed up the beach. In a low, worried voice, Katie's mom explained to her husband what had happened to the ski.

"This was no equipment failure," Mr. Cobb said seriously. Nancy nodded. "Someone had to have done this on purpose—someone like Miller Burton," he added bitterly. "He's got to be the one behind all this. The man is obsessed with stopping Katie."

Nancy hesitated before she replied. She was suspicious of Miller Burton, but they needed proof. How could he have gotten access to the ski? And who else could have obtained the Blue Waters stationery that Katie's warning note had been typed on?

83

Reserving judgment, Nancy merely said to Mr. Cobb, "Burton definitely needs to be checked out."

"Checked out?" Mr. Cobb said impatiently. "I think Burton needs to be locked away. Who knows what his next plan includes—maybe blowing up a boat." He stalked off to the umbrella to join Bridget, who was sitting, calmly observing the group.

As Nancy watched Mr. Cobb, she realized that the stress of the last twenty-four hours was getting to him. She understood how worried he was about Katie. She, too, wanted to find out who was after Katie, but she couldn't accuse Burton without proof.

For the next hour or so Nancy, Bess, and George watched the trick competition from the shore. The eight competitors—Katie and Jackie included—were locked in a tight battle. The crowd was treated to a dazzling display of footwork and legwork.

In the end Katie, Jackie, and Pam qualified for the final round, along with one other skier, Margot Adler. Their scores were close, but Katie's tricks had given her a slight edge.

Pat McKiernan stood at the front of the tournament tent with his electronic bullhorn. "That ends our second day of competition," he announced. "And things are really heating up. Especially for the overall title where Katie Cobb

84

and Pam Cartwright are our only two remaining competitors.

"Everything comes down to the final performances," he continued. "You won't want to miss it! Thanks for coming. We'll see you all tomorrow."

Nancy, Bess, and George found the Cobbs packing up their gear. Katie was happy but exhausted. Jackie was sitting on a nearby blanket, talking to Katie. "We're heading back to the cabin," Katie said to the girls. "What do you have planned?"

"Do you feel up to having some visitors?" Nancy asked gently. She had several questions to ask—whether the slashed ski had been mislaid in the past day, and whether anyone had seen Gary Trachok around the beach before the slalom event. Nancy had noticed that Gary stuck close to Pam during the trick competition.

Katie shook her head. "You know I'd love to spend some time relaxing with you guys, but if I don't get a nap, I can kiss this tournament goodbye. I'm beat."

Nancy nodded sympathetically. "We'll catch up with you later," she said.

"How about joining us for dinner?" Mrs. Cobb asked. "We plan on grilling hamburgers tonight."

"Sounds great," George said. "Thank you. Maybe we can spend the rest of the day checking out tourist attractions."

"How about Donner Lake?" Bridget piped up.

"Uh, thanks for the suggestion, Bridget," Nancy said.

Bridget shrugged. "It's fun, and it's less crowded than this dumb beach. At least it isn't overrun with water-skiers from this obnoxious tournament."

"Great," George said brightly. "Who knows? Maybe we can get Bess on skis."

Donner Lake, a short distance west of Truckee, was much smaller than Lake Tahoe. But as Nancy, Bess, and George drove into the parking lot at the east end of the lake, they could see the water was crowded with ski boats, sailboats, and jet skis.

"All ready, Bess?" George asked with enthusiasm as they left the car. Katie had recommended that Bess take a lesson from a private instructor at Donner Lake. Bess had spent the forty-five-minute drive to Donner Lake talking excitedly about her lesson. She had been imagining how she'd look cutting across the lake on a sleek slalom ski.

Now as the three girls stood on the small patch of beach, Bess nervously eyed the water where other skiers whizzed by behind power boats.

"I don't know," she said, biting her lip. "What if I fall? I'm not so good at this."

"Everybody falls." George grinned. "If you do,

you'll just get wet. It's better than falling off your bike," she pointed out.

Nancy was admiring the pine-covered mountains cut through near the top by train tracks. A train was weaving its way in and out of the mountains, disappearing into snow tunnels every once in a while. Now she turned to Bess.

"You'd hate to pass up this opportunity," she reminded her. "When will you have this chance again?"

Bess hesitated for a moment and then said in a small voice, "Okay. But if I want to stop, then I stop—no questions or pleading." She gave Nancy and George a warning look.

They both nodded. "Fair enough," George said.

A few minutes later the three were speaking to Derek, a ski instructor whose name they had gotten at the ski-rental office. Nancy could tell that once Bess had seen Derek's dark hair, tanned skin, and rugged good looks, she'd begin to like the idea of skiing better.

From a small dock nearby George and Derek's driver climbed into his boat. They drove over to the section of water designated for beginning skiers to go over the basics. Meanwhile Nancy stood with Bess on the shoreline, helping her adjust the boots on a pair of skis. Derek stood with them, giving Bess instructions.

"First and most important," Derek said, "you

need to relax. All you have to do is sit back on the skis and let the boat pull you. The boat should do the work."

Bess nodded attentively, and Derek continued. "The second thing to remember is to keep your arms straight and your knees bent." He handed Bess a small life vest, and she put it on, attaching the buckles in front. Then he waded into the water with the two skis and waved to the boat waiting for them.

George tossed out a rope, and Derek caught it. He turned to Bess. "Okay, let's go," he said.

Bess's eyes popped open. "Now?" she said. "You've only given me two pointers."

Derek grinned. "The best way to learn is by doing it," he said.

Bess gave Nancy a panicky look and stepped gingerly into the cold water. She held her arms up to keep them from feeling the shock of the cool water temperature.

Derek helped Bess slip the ski on her right foot. Bess stuck her leg straight out, and the top of the ski wobbled awkwardly above the water. "Now sit down so we can put the left ski on," Derek said.

"In the water?" Bess asked.

Derek laughed. "That's where you'll be skiing. Don't worry, the ski vest should hold you up."

Bess squatted down, lifting her left leg up and floating in a sitting position. As she did, the ski on her right foot flopped around, and she paddled desperately with her hands to keep her balance. The life vest had inched up when she sat, and now the tops of the armholes came up to her ears.

"How will I ever stand up in these?" Bess wailed. "I can't even sit."

Nancy smiled from the shore, remembering when she was first water-skiing. She waded out to Bess and held her friend upright while Derek slipped on the left ski. Then Derek handed Bess the handle attached to the tow rope. Bess grabbed it, still trying to keep her skis straight as she sat in the water.

"Bend your legs," Derek said, pushing her knees up. "And keep the tips of the skis above the surface of the water." Bess struggled to get into position with Nancy holding her from behind.

"Now lean back," Derek said, "and when the boat pulls you, keep leaning back and keep your legs bent." Bess nodded, quietly concentrating.

"Ready?" Nancy asked.

"I guess," Bess whispered.

Derek waved his arm at the boat, and the driver put the boat in gear. The rope pulled Bess's arms, and her body began to rise out of the water. But instead of leaning back, she followed her arms, lurching forward. The rope jerked from her hands, and she fell headfirst, tangling her skis behind her.

Bess pulled her head up, spitting lake water

from her nose and mouth. She squirmed about, trying to get her legs back underneath her. As Nancy helped her to turn over, Bess said, "Okay, that's it. Back to shore."

Derek smiled. "Not so fast. You haven't even gotten the feel of the skis yet." He helped Bess back into her crouched sitting position and waved at the boat. George had gathered up the rope when Bess fell, and now she threw it back to Derek.

Derek handed the rope to Bess. "Now, this time, lean back—way back—and keep your knees bent."

Bess's teeth chattered, and she wiped a strand of wet hair from her face. "But it's cold," she started, "and I—"

"Okay!" Derek yelled to the driver. The boat took off, and a surprised Bess was pulled by her arms again. This time she held her body back, as Derek had said. She began to rise out of the water as the boat picked up speed, and soon she was standing, teetering awkwardly on the two skis.

"She's doing it!" Nancy cried excitedly. She watched as Bess was pulled a few more yards, her knees bent and her legs wide apart. Bess jerked the rope up and down with her outstretched arms as she bounced shakily over the water's surface. In the next instant Nancy saw Bess's arms snap up sharply as she hit a wave in the water. The skis flew out from under her, and she was down.

"Ooh, too bad," Derek said. "But I'm not going to let her give up." He dove into the chest-high water and swam out to Bess, who was about ten yards out. Nancy watched him help Bess put her skis back on—they had come off in the fall.

In a flash Derek had Bess back into position in the deeper water, ready to go again. In seconds the boat was pulling Bess to her feet again. This time Bess leaned back in her crouch, holding herself up over the choppy surface of the lake.

When Nancy saw that Bess had gone about twenty-five yards, she smiled to herself and clapped. Bess was really doing it! Nancy turned to wade back to the shore, out of the cold water.

As she got to the beach a movement in the parking lot, about a hundred yards beyond, caught her eye. Nancy turned toward the gray car the girls were renting.

Someone was walking around the back of the car to the driver's side. The figure was dressed in white shorts and a T-shirt, with dark sunglasses and a baseball cap pulled down low. The person was of medium height, but Nancy couldn't tell if it was a man or a woman.

As Nancy watched, the suspicious figure quickly peered both ways and then bent over the door on the driver's side. Nancy could see a white sleeve moving up and down above the door.

Someone was breaking into their car!

10

True Confessions

Nancy sprinted across the beach to the parking lot. As she reached the edge of the lot, the person crouching by her car saw her.

The figure ducked behind the car and then began to scuttle away, hidden from Nancy.

"Hey!" Nancy yelled. She began running across the pebbly dirt-covered parking lot, but her feet were bare and she had to step carefully. The figure she was chasing obviously had shoes on, because whoever it was moved much more swiftly than Nancy could.

Nancy had almost reached the car when she heard another car door slam. A motor was started, and a black sedan skidded out in reverse from the farthest space.

Stopping abruptly, Nancy peered toward the

car. Unfortunately, the baseball cap made it impossible to see the driver's face.

The car was slammed into Drive and peeled out to the main road, becoming lost in a cloud of dust. The would-be thief had escaped—and Nancy hadn't even caught the license plate number!

Nancy turned away from the main road, frustrated. There was no one else in the small parking lot. She picked her way across the pebbly dirt to her car.

Trying the driver's door, she found that it was still locked—the person apparently had not been able to open the door. The paint by the keyhole had been badly scraped, though.

Nancy bent down, searching the door and ground for any clue. She found nothing but pebbles, pine needles, and dirt.

Nancy walked slowly back to the beach, the hot afternoon sun warming her face. She wondered why someone had tried to break into her car. It could have been an ordinary thief, but she doubted that an experienced car thief would break into a car in broad daylight.

What if the figure in white knew whose car it was? Nancy thought uneasily. That meant the person had targeted Nancy, Bess, and George. And if so, Nancy had to assume, it was because of the girls' connection to Katie.

Maybe whoever was after Katie had just paid Nancy a visit, too!

Nancy's heart beat a little faster. She thought of the person who'd been in the sailboat with her in Tahoe City. Was it the same person? She sighed, disappointed that the culprit had slipped away.

When Nancy got back to the little stretch of beach, George and Bess were just climbing out of Derek's boat onto the dock. As Bess thanked Derek and said goodbye to him, her blue eyes were dancing.

"That was great!" Bess gushed to George and Nancy as they left the dock. "It was like I was walking on water. Even though I fell again at the end and had to get a ride in, it was fun."

George smiled at her cousin, shaking her head. "Who'd have thought we'd ever get you to admit that waterskiing was fun?" she said.

Bess laughed. "I think I'm ready to lie on the sand," she confessed, wrapping herself in the towel George had handed her. As they found a spot on the beach, George turned to Nancy. "I saw you running up to the parking lot. What was up?"

"Someone was trying to break into our car," Nancy told Bess and George calmly.

"What?" Bess froze.

"Don't worry," Nancy reassured her as they sat

down on the sand. "He—or she—saw me coming and ran away before the door was opened. I didn't see who it was. Though I did see that he or she was driving a black car. But you know, I am worried that it might have something to do with Katie."

"You mean, whoever is after her is after us now?" Bess asked anxiously.

"Possibly," Nancy said. "I know that there are a few people who aren't happy to see Katie in the tournament. Gary Trachok seems pretty bitter about being fired. Miller Burton is angry at Katie, and Bridget seems to hate being at the tournament," Nancy said, thinking out loud. "It could be that someone knows we're trying to help Katie and wants to stop us."

"What do we do now?" George asked.

"Well, we know it couldn't have been Bridget," Nancy replied. "She's not old enough to drive. But I would like to find out what kind of cars Gary Trachok and Miller Burton drive. I'm sorry, but I think we have to get going. I know we just sat down, but . . ." Nancy stood and shook out her towel. "If I drop you two off at Sand Harbor, could you find Gary Trachok's car?" she asked. "Meanwhile I think I'll check out the Blue Waters office in Incline Village."

"Let's go," George agreed, pulling on a T-shirt over her suit.

Bess sighed. "I think I had more fun falling off my skis," she said.

After she had dropped Bess and George at Sand Harbor, Nancy headed to Incline Village to find the Blue Waters office. Studying the map they had bought, Nancy turned up a steep side street next to a large supermarket. A little way up the street she found the address, a small brick office building. She pulled into the parking lot in back.

As she got out of her gray car, Nancy looked around the parking lot. Several cars were there, but she couldn't tell if any of them belonged to Miller Burton. None of them was black.

Nancy went to the front of the building. A list of offices posted by the door showed that Blue Waters was on the second floor. Nancy climbed the carpeted staircase. At the top was a plain wooden door with Blue Waters painted on it in block letters.

She knocked at the door. There was no reply. Nancy could hear people laughing in an office down the hall. It was about four-thirty so she figured people must still be working. She waited a few seconds before knocking again and calling out, "Mr. Burton?" Still no answer.

Nancy glanced up and down the hallway and then tried the doorknob. It turned easily. She pushed the door open slowly and poked her head in first.

The lights were on in the small office. She saw a large wooden desk, an old metal filing cabinet, and a few molded plastic orange chairs, which looked as if they had been used in a doctor's waiting room. A computer sat on the large desk, and sloppy stacks of papers were piled over the desktop and on the carpeted floor.

"Hello?" Nancy called. When no one answered, she opened the door fully and stepped in. She looked around and noticed an open door on one side of the room.

Peeking through it, she saw another office, a smaller version of the one she was in. Shelves filled with books and papers lined two walls. A large map of Lake Tahoe was pinned to a third wall.

Nancy turned back to the main room. A mug half full of coffee sat on the large desk beside the computer. The computer's screen was on, though it was blank. It looked as though someone had just stepped out of the office for a moment. Nancy moved quickly to take advantage of having the office to herself.

She pulled the warning note to Katie from her pocket. She could tell by the type that it had been written on a typewriter, not a computer. Glancing back into the smaller office, Nancy saw a typewriter sitting on a table.

Hurrying over to the typewriter, Nancy grabbed a piece of paper from a stack next to the table and slid it into the machine. She typed out the words *get out now*, which had been on the note, and rolled the paper up.

Holding the warning note next to the paper in the typewriter, she studied the two side by side. It took her only seconds to realize that the note was typed on a different typewriter. The type size of the office typewriter was much smaller than that on the note.

She rolled the paper out, thinking hard. If Miller Burton *had* typed the note, he hadn't done it at his office. There was also the possibility that Burton was being framed. Someone else could have typed the note on Blue Waters stationery, knowing that Burton's antics would make him appear to be an obvious culprit. If Nancy could enter the office unnoticed, it would be easy for anyone to sneak in and steal the stationery.

Nancy snapped out of her reverie. Someone, maybe Burton, could come back at any moment, and she didn't want to be caught in the office. She did want to question Burton, but being caught snooping wasn't the best way to start.

Putting both pieces of paper in her pocket, Nancy crept back into the larger office. She checked to see if she had overlooked anything of significance. She figured it would look suspicious to sneak out of the office, so she calmly opened the door and strode into the hallway, closing it firmly behind her. There was still no one in the hall. She made her way down the stairs, breathing a sigh of relief.

Back at Sand Harbor Nancy picked up Bess and George. "How did you do?" Nancy asked.

"Not too well," George said. "Pat McKiernan was about the only person from the tournament left on the beach. He said Trachok had just left before we got there."

"But he told us he thinks Trachok drives a red Jeep," Bess added.

"What about you?" George asked. "Did you learn anything at Burton's office?"

Nancy shook her head. "Nothing much. I checked out the typewriter, though. Katie's warning note couldn't have been typed on it."

"So Burton didn't write the note?" Bess asked.

"I can't say that," Nancy replied. "All I know is that it wasn't typed at his office."

In a few minutes they were back in their cabin at Incline Village. While each girl took her turn in the shower, the other two relaxed in front of the cabin's VCR.

Bess was absorbed in a tape of a romantic old movie, one of several that had been provided with the cabin. "Come on, we're due at the Cobbs' for dinner in five minutes," George reminded her, standing impatiently by the cabin's front door.

99

"But we're just getting to the good part," Bess protested. "The hero is about to sweep the heroine off her feet."

Nancy laughed, pulling her friend up off the sofa. "You can watch the ending tonight when we get home."

The three girls decided to walk the half mile to the Cobbs' cabin. Katie greeted them at the door, looking rested and cheerful. "How was the skiing?" she asked Bess. "Do I have a new competitor to worry about?"

Bess smiled. "Not yet. But I can see why you like it so much."

"When everything works, there's nothing better," Katie agreed.

She led them through the cabin to the back deck where Mr. and Mrs. Cobb were standing over a smoking grill. They greeted the girls. "I hope you like hamburgers," Mr. Cobb said. "They're my specialty."

They all nodded, and Nancy held up a plastic container. "I brought dessert," she said. "Just cookies—but they're Hannah Gruen's secret-recipe chocolate chip cookies. She baked them for us before we came to Tahoe. She hoped that they would bring Katie luck."

"My favorite!" Katie remembered. "And Bridget's, too—that is, if she's eating tonight," she added, her face falling a bit. She took the cookies from Bess. "I think dinner's about ready. We're going to eat out here."

Mr. and Mrs. Cobb emerged from the smoke to put a plate of hamburgers on the picnic table. Bridget joined the group, and in a few minutes they were all eating hamburgers and potato salad.

Nancy watched Bridget carefully. The young girl was smiling and attentive as Bess talked about her skiing adventure. But when Katie spoke—or when anyone mentioned Katie's skiing—she immediately closed up.

Nancy suspected that Bridget was jealous of the attention given to Katie. She wondered how deep the jealousy went. Would Bridget actually try to hurt Katie?

As they finished eating, Mrs. Cobb suggested they move indoors for dessert since the mountain air was growing cold. Settling into the cozy living room, they all helped themselves to Hannah's cookies.

Mr. Cobb came in last, with a videotape in his hand. "How would you girls like to see yourselves on TV?" he asked, popping the tape in the video recorder.

"Oh, good," Bridget said sarcastically, slumping down in her chair, "more skiing to watch."

"You're on here, too," Mr. Cobb said, pushing the Start button. "In fact, I think just about everyone is."

The tape began with the Cobbs' arrival at the beach that morning for the slalom run. Mr. Cobb was right, Nancy thought. Just about everybody on the beach seemed to have been taped.

The girls giggled as they watched an angry Gary Trachok yank on Pam Cartwright, who was waving at the camera. He hurried her off with a scowl. They saw themselves walking to the beach from the parking lot.

The video then showed the shoreline and the buzz of activity as skiers and drivers prepared for the slalom run. As the camera slowly zoomed to the boat Katie used, Bridget suddenly sat up. "Dad, haven't we seen enough?" she said quickly. "I mean, I'm sure this is boring for Nancy, Bess, and George."

"Oh, no," Bess put in. "It's fun."

The tape continued, but now Bridget was sitting on the edge of her seat, glancing nervously from the screen to her parents. The camera panned to the right of the boat where they watched Bridget come into view. She was standing with her back to the camera, in shallow water next to the boat. She obviously didn't know she was being taped. She was bent over, her hands on some object in front of her.

Nancy sat up, staring intently at the tape. As the camcorder continued to pan to the right, Bridget's back came into better focus. "Can you stop the tape for a moment?" Nancy asked Mr. Cobb.

"Sure," he said, hitting the Pause button. "What is it?"

"I'm not sure," Nancy murmured, standing up to take a closer look at the television screen.

She gazed at the frozen image, which had captured Bridget bent over in the water next to the boat. Nancy could have sworn Bridget held her sister's . . .

Suddenly Bridget jumped to her feet. "Okay, okay, I'll tell you!" she cried. Nancy turned to gaze at the girl.

"What is this about?" Mrs. Cobb said.

Katie was peering at her sister with a puzzled frown.

Bridget's face was bright red as she turned to her mother and blurted out, "I'm the one who slashed Katie's ski boot!"

11

Surprises in the Night

Mr. and Mrs. Cobb stared at their daughter, dumbstruck. Bess's jaw was hanging open as she and George watched Katie's reaction.

"What did you say?" Mr. Cobb asked, finding his voice.

Bridget was close to tears. She lowered her eyes and said in a shaky voice, "I was the one who cut Katie's ski boot so she couldn't use the ski." She raised her eyes to Nancy's. "You knew, didn't you?"

Nancy was still standing by the television screen with the frozen image of Bridget next to the boat. "I had wondered," she admitted. "Especially just now, watching the tape. That's what you're doing here, isn't it?" she said, pointing to Bridget on the screen.

Bridget nodded. "I knew that was why you wanted to pause the tape."

"Bridget, how could you?" Mrs. Cobb blurted out. "What if Katie had tried to use that ski? She could have been badly hurt! And what if we hadn't had another ski?"

"And what about that release rope stunt?" Mr. Cobb put in angrily. "That—"

"I had nothing to do with that!" Bridget cried, her eyes wide. "I don't know who's been doing the other stuff."

The room was silent. Bridget looked from one face to the next.

"I swear!" she said. "I was with you guys when that happened. I know you don't believe me, but all I did was cut that boot. I was just so mad. . . ." she said, her voice trailing off.

"At what?" Katie asked quietly. She had been watching Bridget closely, her face a mixture of hurt and confusion.

Bridget's eyes were welling up with tears. "I'm sorry, Katie, I really am. It's just that I get so tired of hearing about you all the time—going to *your* tournaments, buying *your* equipment, talking about *your* practices. . . .

"This morning I felt like I was going to burst. I started to think I'd never have one moment for me." Bridget paused. "I didn't want to hurt you. I thought as soon as you put on the ski you'd figure out what was wrong."

"But why didn't you just talk to me?" Katie said.

"I tried," Bridget said. "I say stuff all the time to you and Mom and Dad. But everyone ignores me—or treats me like a baby." She dropped unhappily back into her chair.

"Well, when you act like a baby, what do you expect?" Mr. Cobb said in exasperation.

"Dad!" Katie said. "I think Bridget has a point. We *do* spend a lot of time on my skiing."

Nancy turned to Bridget. "So you haven't been involved in anything except cutting Katie's ski?" she asked carefully.

Bridget started to nod, then halted. "Oh, I almost forgot—that was me you chased through the woods this morning. I was watching you and Katie poke around the deck. When you heard me, I didn't want you to know I was spying on you, so I took off running."

"Do you know anything about the warning note we found there?" Nancy asked her.

Bridget acted confused. "What warning note? I didn't even know that Katie had heard someone at her window until I heard you talking."

Nancy frowned. She believed Bridget was telling the truth. That meant that someone else was responsible for moving the ski fin, jamming the release rope and leaving the warning note—not to mention pushing her in the water and attempting to break into the car. Nancy still didn't know who that someone was.

Everyone in the room had fallen silent. Mr. and Mrs. Cobb were obviously upset by Bridget's confession, and Nancy felt that they had to have some privacy. She turned to Bess and George. "I think it's time for us to get back to our cabin," she suggested.

Bess and George stood up at once, understanding Nancy's meaning immediately.

"Mr. Cobb, could I borrow your videotapes overnight?" Nancy asked. "Maybe they contain a clue I've overlooked."

"Sure," he said. He popped out the tape they had been watching and gave Nancy the tape from the previous day as well. Nancy, George, and Bess then thanked the Cobbs for dinner, and Katie walked them to the door.

"I'm sorry about all this," she said. "I guess Bridget and I have a lot of talking to do."

Nancy smiled. "There's no need to apologize. We'll see you tomorrow at the beach."

Katie nodded. "Jackie and I are going to do a practice run in the morning. You're welcome to watch. The beach is usually quiet early in the morning."

The girls thanked her and stepped out into the dark, cool night. Bess zipped up her sweatshirt and they walked off the wooden deck onto the gravel driveway.

They had walked a couple of steps when Bess said, "I can't believe Bridget would—"

Nancy suddenly put her hand up, motioning Bess to be quiet. The three girls stopped. Bess and George peered at Nancy in the darkness.

"What is it?" George whispered.

Nancy turned her head, listening carefully. She was sure she had heard something move on the gravel near the end of the driveway.

As the three girls stood there silently, barely breathing, a faint crunching sound could be heard just ahead of them. Nancy was certain that someone was walking up the driveway.

Moving slowly, Nancy crept behind the Cobbs' large car. She motioned to Bess and George to move behind the car as well. Then she tiptoed around to the end of the car and peered around the side.

"Oh!" she gasped, startled.

Two piercing eyes glared at Nancy from out of the darkness. She found herself inches away from Miller Burton.

Nancy caught her breath again. Miller's tall frame loomed over her.

Burton let out a surprised gasp, too. "You again!" he said, squinting at Nancy.

"What are you doing here?" Nancy asked briskly. She heard Bess and George move up behind her.

Burton held up his hand, clutching a pile of

papers. "I'm trying to educate people like you," he said. "These fliers will tell people how Tahoe has been affected by drought conditions over the last several years."

"You're passing out fliers at night?" George asked skeptically.

Burton scowled at her. "What kind of response do you think I'd get if I did it during the day?" he said. "I'd probably have those sheriff's deputies after me again."

The girls watched him walk to the front of the Cobbs' car and slap a flier on the windshield, pinning it in place with the wiper. He came back. "This way people have to see our message before they go anywhere," he said.

"Is there some reason you've chosen this car?" Nancy queried Burton carefully.

"I've put a flier on every car on this street," Burton answered. "And on the three streets before this one." He glanced at the Cobbs' car. "This one probably belongs to vacationers, just like the others," he added, shaking his head.

If Burton *did* know this was the Cobbs' car, he was doing a very good job of pretending he didn't, Nancy thought.

As the tall bearded man turned to go, Nancy said quickly, "I thought those deputies arrested you this afternoon."

Burton let out a short laugh. "Nah. They just gave me a warning, like they always do." Then his eyes narrowed. "First you almost tackle me at the beach, and now you're giving me the third degree. Who are you? And what have you got against me?"

Nancy drew herself up. "Let's just say I'm Katie Cobb's friend," she said evenly. "And I don't like the way you've been treating her."

"Cobb? Oh, the skier," Burton said, trying to place Katie's name.

"Yes—the skier you've been threatening," Bess blurted out.

Burton seemed a bit confused. "The only thing I'm threatening is the tournament's use of the lake. And Katie Cobb stands to profit from it. So obviously I want to draw attention to that." He shrugged. "It's nothing personal."

Nancy eyed the man closely. Burton seemed to be telling the truth, but she needed proof. "Where were you last night?" she asked, thinking about the tournament dinner and the attempted break-in.

Burton was losing patience. "Who do you think you are, a detective or something?" he said, glaring down at Nancy. Then, stroking his beard, he added, "Not that it's any of your business, but I was at a Blue Waters strategy meeting. The other members can vouch for me."

He turned around, the fliers cradled in one arm, and began walking down the driveway. Then he stopped suddenly and came back. Without a word, he handed Nancy, Bess, and George each a flier. A slight grin stole across his face as he mumbled, "Some bedtime reading for you." Then he walked on down the dark street.

"Well!" George said in surprise when Burton was out of earshot. "He's persistent, isn't he?"

Nancy nodded slowly, thinking about this chance meeting with Miller Burton. It was quite a coincidence. Burton seemed to have an alibi for the night before, but he did act more interested in the lake than in Katie. Still the coincidence was too great, and Nancy couldn't dismiss him as a suspect yet.

"Why don't we talk about it at the cabin?" Bess said, folding her arms across her white sweatshirt. "I'm freezing—and I want to get back to my movie."

The three began the walk back, heading in the opposite direction from Burton. They passed beneath the lone streetlight, where moths flickered in and out of the faint glow.

"I hope the Cobbs can work things out with Bridget," Bess said quietly. "I can't help but feel sorry for her."

"But if Bridget swears she only cut the boot, and Burton is providing alibis for himself, then who's after Katie?" George asked. "Who tried to break into the car? Gary Trachok?"

"That's just what I was wondering," Nancy admitted. "Whoever altered Katie's ski fin and

111

jammed the release rope knew something about skiing. Whoever left the note knows where the Cobbs are staying. And if that's the same person who also tried to break into our car, then he or she probably followed us to Donner Lake."

Bess shivered. "Sounds like Gary Trachok."

Hearing a car approach from behind, Nancy stepped onto the shoulder of the road, deep in thought. George and Bess did the same, walking single file so the car could pass. Now that they had moved out from under the streetlight, the night was so dark they could hardly see.

The sound of the oncoming car was getting louder, and Nancy realized it had to be going pretty fast.

Something was strange, though. Where were the lights? Although the engine's roar indicated the car was almost next to them, no headlights lit up the road.

Then Nancy saw a huge hulking shape burst from the darkness. She gasped.

There *was* a car, and it was right behind them—barreling down on them dead-on!

12

The Camera Never Lies

"Watch out!" Nancy yelled, whipping her head around. She pushed Bess back from the shoulder, hearing her startled cry as she knocked into George.

Nancy could feel the heat from the car's engine as she flung herself onto the hard dirt and rolled back off the shoulder. For a moment it felt as if she were moving in slow motion. She listened to Bess and George hit the ground and roll, too.

The roaring of the engine passed within inches of Nancy's head, and she could feel the vibration from the tires as they skidded past her body, kicking up rocks and dirt.

Nancy held her breath as the car sped past, the sound of the engine soon lost in the distance.

Nancy let out the breath she had been holding.

Pulling herself up slowly, she brushed dirt from her jeans and shook it out of her hair. "Are you two all right?" she asked Bess and George.

"I think so," Bess said, climbing to her knees. Nancy gave her a hand to help her up.

"My heart's going a mile a minute," George said, "and I think I've got a thorn stuck in my palm, but other than that I'm fine." She got to her feet and stared down the road angrily. "That driver barely missed us. How careless can you get?"

"Pretty careless, if you don't use your headlights," Nancy observed thoughtfully. She caught sight of the videotapes, which she had dropped when she dove at Bess. She picked them up, hoping the film hadn't been damaged.

"No headlights!" Bess exclaimed, standing up. "No wonder the driver didn't see us."

"Maybe the driver *did* see us," Nancy said.

George slowly said, "That means that car was deliberately trying to hit us."

"We could have been killed!" Bess moaned.

Nancy nodded. "I know. I mean, we have no *proof* that this was done on purpose," she said. "But driving too fast down a dark street with no lights on and swerving into people who are walking on the shoulder hardly seems accidental."

"Did you get a look at the car?" George asked.

Nancy shook her head. "I didn't see it until it

was right on top of us, but I think it was black. I can't be sure."

"Do you think Miller Burton came back for us?" George asked.

Before Nancy could answer, Bess said nervously, "Can we get home before we find ourselves in the middle of another accident?" She glanced around at the dark woods around them and shuddered.

When the three finished their walk home, Bess said she was too tired to watch her movie. George went to bed soon after Bess. Nancy went to her room, but even though every part of her body was worn out, her mind was racing.

She couldn't stop from thinking about all that had happened—and wondering what was going to happen. The next day was the last day of the tournament, and whoever was after Katie was still at large. Now that person seemed to be after Nancy, Bess, and George, too! The near-miss with the car seemed to confirm that.

Tossing on her bed, Nancy knew she had to be overlooking something—a clue or a connection. She just hoped it would come to her—before it was too late.

Nancy blinked her eyes open the next morning. Sun filtered in through her window shutters. Was it morning already? She couldn't remember when she had finally fallen asleep.

The clock beside the bed read 6:32 A.M. Nancy pulled on her robe and padded out to the living room. The cabin was silent. She figured Bess and George must still be asleep.

Sitting down on the couch, Nancy found herself picking up where she had left off the night before, thinking about the tournament.

Then she noticed Mr. Cobb's videotapes sitting on the side table. Maybe seeing the tournament from the beginning would trigger some fresh idea, she thought.

She popped the first tape into the video recorder, rewound the tape, and hit Play.

The video began with a beautiful panoramic shot of Lake Tahoe. Nancy could tell that Mr. Cobb must have been filming from the back of the beach area at the Sand Harbor boat launch. The time in the corner of the screen read 7:50— at least a couple of hours before the official start of the tournament two days ago. There had been few people on the beach at that time.

Nancy watched as the camera panned down the beach. Katie was coming out of the water, carrying her slalom ski. She waved and smiled at the camera. Nancy heard Mr. Cobb say, "How was the practice run?" Katie gave him a thumbs-up sign. Then she pointed down the beach and said, "Jackie's going now."

The camera panned toward the takeoff area,

116

where Jackie Albert was standing knee-deep in the water. As the camera zoomed closer to her, she turned and waved, calling, "Wish me luck!" to Mr. Cobb.

Nancy sat up, staring at the television. Then she jumped up and stopped the tape, rewinding it briefly. Kneeling in front of the television, she watched Jackie turn and wave again. Nancy's heart was pounding in her chest.

Jackie was wearing a ski glove—a black ski glove with a pink neon stripe. It looked identical to the one Nancy had found in Katie's boat after the release rope jammed!

Nancy hit the Pause button. Then she ran to get the glove from her room. Holding it in her hand, she reran the tape, peering closely at Jackie's glove.

The pink-and-black glove on the tape was identical to the one Nancy was now holding.

Nancy frowned, trying to remember if she had seen Jackie wear a glove like that during the tournament. She couldn't have worn it, Nancy thought—not if she had lost it in Katie's boat.

Nancy quickly popped out the tape and re-placed it with the second day's tape. She pressed the Fast Forward button until the image of Jackie Albert appeared on the screen. Nancy gasped— Jackie's hand was gloveless!

Nancy's skin was tingling. Jackie Albert?

Could she have been the one who jammed a pin in the release mechanism? Could she have tampered with the fin on Katie's slalom ski?

Staring at the tape, Nancy realized that Jackie had had a perfect opportunity during the early morning practice run. She could easily have gotten into Katie's boat to set up the two "accidents" before the beach became crowded.

Now that Nancy thought about it, she remembered several things Jackie had said to point Nancy in the direction of Gary Trachok. And Jackie could have planted the warning note to blame the mishaps on Miller Burton—she had seen how much the environmentalist bothered the Cobbs. She probably thought it would be easy to throw the suspicion on him.

Why would Jackie try to hurt Katie? Nancy wondered. According to Katie, the two were old friends. Katie said Jackie had even taught her her first ski tricks.

Then Nancy reminded herself that Katie was beating Jackie in trick now—Jackie's only event. If Katie was forced out of the competition, Jackie would almost surely win the trick division.

Then Nancy's eyes popped open, and she jumped to her feet. The night before Katie had said that she and Jackie were going for a practice run this morning. That meant they would be together at the beach right now.

If Nancy was right about Jackie, then this

would be Jackie's last opportunity to knock Katie out of the competition!

Nancy hadn't a moment to lose. She ran into her room and threw on some shorts and then quickly scribbled a note to Bess and George. She slipped quietly out the door and jumped into her rental car. The road to Sand Harbor was deserted at that time of the morning.

As Nancy pulled into the boat launch parking lot, there were only two other cars there. Nancy recognized one as the Cobbs' wagon. The other was a black boxy car, just like the one she'd seen speeding away at Donner Lake.

Nancy parked and ran to the top of the beach. She squinted at the long dock, about two hundred yards beyond the stretch of sand.

Katie was lying facedown on the long dock, motionless, and bending over her was Jackie Albert.

Nancy cupped her hands to her mouth and yelled, "Katie!" Katie didn't move, but Jackie turned. Then she bent back over Katie, straining to lift the limp skier.

Nancy realized that Katie must be unconscious. Her head flopped around as Jackie picked her up and moved her toward a boat tied to the wooden pier.

Nancy raced down the beach, her eyes trained on the dock. As she slogged her way through the deep sand, she watched as Jackie heaved Katie into the boat. Jackie then untied the rope mooring the boat to the pier.

Nancy, panting hard, sprinted up to the dock. She jumped onto the wooden planks and ran toward the boat. As she drew near, Jackie whirled around.

Nancy faced the dark-haired skier. Jackie seemed like a different person from the smiling woman Nancy had met two days earlier. Her skin was pale and drawn except for a red flush on her cheeks. Her eyes were narrowed to slits, and her disheveled hair hung in limp strands.

Jackie was out of breath and could barely speak. "I don't know what happened, Nancy. Katie just fainted. I tried to . . ." She paused, taking in the confusion on Nancy's face. "Maybe you should check her out," she suggested.

Nancy raced to the edge of the dock and leaned over to look at Katie.

As she lowered her eyes something struck the back of her head, knocking her to her knees. Before Nancy could catch her breath, Jackie grabbed her by the arm, pulling her back to a sitting position.

Nancy jerked her arm forward and tried to push Jackie away with her free arm, but the skier's anger gave her the advantage of additional strength. She wrenched Nancy's arm behind her back, pressing her weight against it. Nancy cried out in pain.

From the corner of her eye Nancy saw one of Jackie's hands move around, holding a white cloth. Nancy twisted wildly in her sitting position, trying to escape Jackie's grip. She guessed the cloth had been dipped in chloroform.

As Jackie thrust her hand toward Nancy's face, Nancy desperately twisted her head away.

Just then Jackie gave Nancy's arm a violent pull. Nancy gasped, tears coming to her eyes. Pain shot through her right arm.

She saw a shadow cross her face. She caught her breath, and in the next instant, everything went black.

13

Adrift!

Nancy's eyes fluttered open. The sun seemed to be right on top of her, piercing her eyelids. She squinted, trying to see.

She felt as if she were waking from a long sleep. Her brain felt thick and slow and the world seemed to be spinning. Slowly feeling returned to her body.

Her right shoulder began to throb painfully. She knew she was lying down, but her body was so heavy it felt as if she were being pinned down.

Still squinting, she tried to focus on a blurry figure moving above her. Though its back was turned to Nancy, she could tell it was Jackie Albert.

Nancy turned her head to get a better look at the skier. Jackie was bent over halfway, rocking slightly. She pulled herself up with a grunt, lifting something in her arms. Nancy's eyes opened wide. In Jackie's arms was the still unconscious Katie.

Nancy lifted her head slightly, her neck muscles straining. There was water as far as she could see. They were in the boat, which Jackie must have driven out onto Lake Tahoe while she and Katie were unconscious.

Nancy put her head down, tired from the effort of lifting it. She heard the slap of rubber against the water outside the boat. She realized that Jackie was lifting Katie into another vessel of some kind—probably a rubber raft.

Jackie must be planning to transfer her to the raft next, Nancy guessed. Then she would abandon the two of them in the lake!

Nancy closed her eyes again, desperate to focus her muddy thoughts. Now what? If she could gain control of the boat, she and Katie might be able to escape. She'd have to overpower Jackie first, though.

She tried to lift herself onto her left elbow. Her arm shook and the dizziness became more intense. It's no use, she thought, lowering herself. She was too weak to fight the skier.

She saw Jackie rise, having placed Katie in the raft. She would turn to Nancy in seconds. Nancy quickly searched the boat for a weapon.

Wedged into the side compartment next to her, Nancy noticed a short red tube. She wrapped her hand around it, hoping it was what she thought it was—a flare. It wasn't much of a weapon, but it could come in handy. She shoved it into her pocket and closed her eyes just before Jackie turned back to her.

Nancy let her body go limp, hoping Jackie would think she was still unconscious. She felt Jackie's arms wriggle under her body. Then Jackie slowly lifted Nancy, swaying as she turned to the other side of the boat.

Nancy was half-placed, half-thrown into the rubber raft. A dank, musty smell hit her immediately, and she felt herself bobbing in the water.

She heard Jackie breathing heavily in the boat nearby. In a few seconds the boat's motor started up with a deep gurgle. The engine roared loudly for a moment. Then the raft was rocked by the wake and waves from the boat. The engine's noise grew fainter and fainter as the boat sped off.

When the engine sound had died away completely, Nancy opened her eyes and struggled up to a sitting position. The lake stretched out endlessly in all directions. Nancy had no idea where they were, and there were no boats in sight.

She looked down at Katie, who was lying still, breathing deeply. Her arms were pinned against her sides because of the way Jackie had dumped her. One leg was shoved awkwardly against the side of the raft. Using her left arm, Nancy straightened Katie's arms and moved her leg, trying to get her into a more comfortable position.

She heard a low moan and saw Katie's eyelids begin to flutter. The skier automatically drew her hand up to shade her eyes from the sun. Then she shook her head as if to clear it.

"Katie?" Nancy said.

Katie slowly turned toward Nancy. She rubbed her eyes, trying to bring them into focus. "Nancy?" she said, her voice thick. She continued to blink and look around. "Wh-where are we?"

Nancy sighed. "Somewhere on the lake," she said.

Katie felt the rubber side of the raft. "In this?" she said.

"In this," Nancy confirmed. "Jackie dumped us out here."

"Oh, yeah—Jackie," Katie said, trying to sit up. After straining for a moment she gave up and slumped back down. "I went down to the beach to meet her for a practice run," Katie said, fighting to remember. "And then—"

"And then she used chloroform to knock both of us out," Nancy finished. "And drove us out here in a boat. She's probably on her way back to the tournament now."

Katie stared at Nancy, looking completely bewildered. "Jackie? Why would Jackie do this?"

Nancy spoke gently to her friend. "She's the

one who's been after you," she said. "I realized it only this morning. I knew she had you at the beach alone, so I drove down to stop her. I caught her putting you in a ski boat." She paused, then said quietly, "I think Jackie finally figured there was only one way to beat you—get rid of you."

Katie was shaking her head as she listened. "No, no. Jackie? She's a friend," Katie said. "Besides, we don't even compete head-to-head anymore."

"But ever since you started skiing competitively, Jackie hasn't been able to win," Nancy pointed out. "She said she switched to trick because it was more fun, but maybe she thought she'd have a better chance at beating you at trick. After all, you had beaten her consistently in slalom.

"And now you're beating her in trick, too," Nancy went on. "She might have been your friend when you first began skiing, but I don't think she is now."

Katie closed her eyes and was silent for a moment. Then she said, "Jackie *is* competitive, I'll admit. But she wouldn't hurt me! Don't forget, someone put a pin in the release mechanism. That could have done more than just put me out of competition—I could have drowned."

Nancy knew it must be difficult for Katie to believe a friend could have betrayed her in such a frightening way. "Jackie had me fooled, too," she admitted. "But I found her glove in your boat at the same time I found the pin. She must have dropped it when she was inserting the pin. Remember your early morning practice run on the first day of the tournament? That was the perfect time for her to set up the accidents."

"So she moved the fin on my ski, too?" Katie asked quietly.

"She could have easily done it that morning," Nancy said. "She was the only one, besides the driver, who had access to the boat and your equipment."

Katie finally pulled herself to a sitting position. Now she nodded slowly, gazing pensively at the lake. "And I guess it was Jackie who tried to break into my room the night before last."

"She probably just wanted to leave that warning note, but you almost caught her," Nancy said. "She wrote the note on the Blue Waters stationery, hoping you'd blame Miller Burton."

Nancy paused for a moment, thinking. "In fact, Jackie was the one who encouraged me to go to Truckee to check up on Miller Burton. She probably thought that would get me out of the way while she checked out your cabin since she planned to break in."

Katie sighed. "Well, that would explain why Jackie seemed so interested in your detective work. She was asking me how successful you had been in solving other cases." She shook her head sadly. "Oh, Nancy, I never would have guessed. I thought Jackie was my friend."

Nancy nodded. "That was what she wanted you to think," she said.

The two girls sat quietly for a moment, gazing at the vast expanse of lake around them as they bobbed in the small raft.

"Well, what now?" Katie said. "We could drift around forever without being seen. Tahoe's the biggest mountain lake in America." Then she stopped and said ruefully, "This is probably not the best time for me to play tour guide."

Nancy reached into her pocket and pulled out the flare. "I grabbed this from the boat," she said, turning it around in her hand. "I hope it works."

Katie's eyes lit up. "Great! Let's give it a shot," she said eagerly.

Nancy frowned, looking around the lake. The water lapped quietly against the raft. "I don't know," Nancy began. "It's still so early—there aren't very many boats out. The water-skiers are probably near the shoreline. I'm afraid there wouldn't be anyone to see the flare if we sent it up now."

Katie nodded. "That's true. We don't want to waste it."

Nancy shifted her position in the pliable raft. She was searching for the nearest shore, wondering if it were possible to swim to land. But nothing was in sight—she and Katie might have to swim for miles. And both of them were still weak from the chloroform.

They couldn't even paddle the raft with their arms, Nancy realized, glancing at her wrenched right arm and noticing there were no paddles in the tiny raft.

All at once Nancy sat straight up, cocking her head.

"What?" Katie asked.

Nancy put her finger to her lips, motioning Katie to be quiet. Then she heard it again—a faint hissing noise. She leaned forward, pressing her ear to the side of the raft. The sound became louder.

Nancy slowly ran her hand along the tubelike side of the raft. Katie watched her, not moving a muscle. Nancy's fingers slid along the rubbery skin, then stopped. The smooth surface was broken by a small snag. Leaving her fingers on it, Nancy put her face right over the spot. Her heart sank.

The snag was actually a small tear about an inch long. The raft had been punctured, and air was rapidly escaping.

Nancy and Katie were sinking!

14

Water, Water Everywhere

Nancy kept her fingers on the small opening and turned slowly to Katie. Katie was staring at the spot Nancy was holding, her eyes wide. "Don't tell me," she said to Nancy. "A hole, right?"

Nancy nodded, and Katie dropped her head in defeat. "Looks like Jackie thought of everything, didn't she?" she said quietly.

"I'm not sure that she cut the raft on purpose," Nancy said, "but it wouldn't surprise me. Look at this puncture—it's a clean slit. If the raft had accidentally caught on something, it probably would have left a jagged tear."

Nancy turned back around, gazing out at the still deserted lake. She was trying to think calmly, fighting down the waves of panic that kept rising. Every second counted. The raft would not hold out much longer. Already it was losing its shape, lying in soft folds where it should have been firm.

Nancy glanced at Katie, whose head was hanging down. Then Katie snapped it back up. "The flare!" she said. "We've got to set it off now, right?"

"Yes," Nancy agreed, desperately hoping that there was a boat nearby.

Katie pulled the release trigger of the flare, and a flash of red went bursting into the sky. Nancy and Katie followed it with their eyes. They kept staring at the sky in hopeful silence, long after the brief flare had disappeared.

The only sounds they could hear were water lapping against the sides of the raft and the air slowly hissing out of the raft.

Minutes crawled by with no sign or sound of a boat. Nancy still had her fingers pressed over the tear. She knew she wasn't stopping the air, but she had to do something.

Katie suddenly looked up. "You know how to swim, right?" she asked, breaking the silence.

Nancy nodded. Katie looked out at the miles of cold lake water surrounding them. Then she lapsed into silence again.

A few more minutes ticked by—maybe five, maybe fifteen, it was hard to tell. Katie had taken off her watch for her morning practice run, and Nancy had left the cabin in such a hurry, she'd forgotten to put hers on. Nancy thought she could tell that the sun had climbed a little higher in the sky.

Katie looked up again. "Well, I guess Jackie got what she wanted," she said glumly. "She's probably preparing for her trick run now. No one will be able to find me, so I'll be disqualified," she said imagining the scene. "Then Jackie will act worried, but she'll compete anyway. Of course, she'll get a good score and win by default. Unless Pam comes up with some good tricks," she added.

"And then Jackie will make a quick exit," Nancy put in. "She won't hang around, answering questions."

"I guess she doesn't expect us to make it back," Katie said, her eyes flashing. "Does she think people will just forget about us—give us up for lost?" Her voice grew angrier as she spoke.

"There's no way that would happen," Nancy said firmly. "Your parents wouldn't stop searching until they found us. And neither would Bess and George. They'll find us eventually."

The two young women couldn't look each other in the eye. In the back of Nancy's mind was a nagging thought—what if they were found too late? How long could they hold out once the raft collapsed? How would they know to look on the lake, anyway? Nancy was sure Katie was thinking the same thing.

Pushing the thought aside, Nancy said with determination, "We have to get back to the beach before the trick competition ends. I don't want Jackie to get away."

Nancy wished her words alone could make it happen.

Time passed. The sun climbed higher. Sweat trickled from Nancy's forehead, and when she wrinkled her nose, she could tell she was getting a sunburn. "We should have brought some of Bess's sunblock," she joked grimly, breaking the heavy silence. Katie managed a wan smile.

Nancy shifted her hips, noticing that she had sunk even lower in the raft. As it continued to lose air, Nancy and Katie were dropping farther and farther into the water.

All at once Katie grabbed Nancy's arm. "Listen," she said. "Do you hear that?"

Nancy sat perfectly still in the raft, listening. She heard nothing.

"I heard a jet ski," Katie said. "I—I . . ." She stopped as a roar echoed clearly in the distance. She nodded her head excitedly, and Nancy began turning in the raft, looking for the sound's source.

Squinting, Nancy peered out over the lake in front of her. Way off, barely visible, was a spray of water. She pointed, and Katie looked toward the far-off dot. The spray came a little closer, and they both saw the jet ski at the same time.

"Over here!" Katie yelled at the top of her lungs. Both girls began waving their arms, clumsily moving to kneeling positions in the raft.

"Hey!" Nancy called out.

The jet ski was turning circles on the lake, apparently oblivious to the raft. The girls waved wildly, Nancy struggling to lift her right arm. They cried out when they heard a lull in the roar.

The person on the jet ski obviously couldn't hear them. With a final sharp turn the jet ski sped off in the opposite direction, leaving only a flash of white spray. The whine of its motor dissolved in the distance.

The girls dropped their arms dejectedly and slumped back into the mushy raft. "Oh, great. Just great," Katie said, her voice tight. "Didn't they see the flare?"

Nancy bit the inside of her cheek. The raft had sunk to within inches of the lake level, and some water had slopped in when the girls had turned to kneel and wave. Nancy leaned back, trying to concentrate.

She had to think of a plan. Holding her fingers against the tear obviously wasn't working. She and Katie had only a few minutes before the raft would completely deflate beneath them.

Once they were dropped into the lake, they would have no choice but to swim. But how long a swim would it be? In which direction should they head?

There had to be another way, Nancy thought. Maybe they could still use the raft in some way, to buoy them up or something. She stared hard at the mountains that loomed in the distance.

As she gazed upward a flash of light suddenly caught her eye, making her blink.

Nancy squinted at the sky. The morning sun was blinding. She dropped her head, wondering if something in the raft had reflected off the sun.

At the same time Katie had lifted her head attentively. She sat very still. Then she whispered to Nancy, "Listen."

Almost at once Nancy heard a dull chopping sound in the distance. The sound came from the sky, and as it neared, Nancy recognized the sound.

It was a helicopter.

Both girls stared at the blue expanse above them. Then Nancy spotted the dull green helicopter. She realized that its rotors glinting in the sun had caused the flash she'd seen.

Nancy and Katie began waving their arms urgently at the helicopter. "Don't leave! Don't leave!" Katie yelled. Nancy prayed that the pilot would somehow see the tiny yellow dot in the vast blue water.

The helicopter was flying toward them, the chopping sound becoming louder. Then Nancy's face broke into a big smile. Printed on the side of the helicopter were the words *Tahoe Rescue Squad.*

Nancy grabbed Katie's arm and pointed at the helicopter. She saw Katie's familiar grin spread across her face.

The helicopter swooped in lower until it was almost directly overhead. The water beneath it ruffled, spreading out in waves from the force of the rotors. Nancy squinted up at the rounded glass front of the helicopter. The pilot nodded at them as he carefully maneuvered the craft above them.

As the helicopter turned Nancy saw that one side was open. A man in a wetsuit dove from the helicopter into the water. At the same time, a cable was dropped from a hoist mounted on the side of the helicopter. A large leather sling was attached to the end of the cable.

The diver swam to the side of the yellow raft. "Are you two okay?" he shouted above the helicopter's roar.

Nancy and Katie both nodded. Kneeling carefully in the soggy, folding raft, the two waited to be lifted.

The diver helped Katie into the sling first, then waved to the helicopter. The cable was slowly hauled up to the open side of the helicopter. Another man helped Katie inside, and the cable was lowered again.

The diver then helped Nancy wrap herself into

the sling. As she reached out to grab it, a stabbing pain shot through her right arm. She held the arm close to her body, struggling to get the sling beneath her.

Finally the diver lifted her into the sling, and Nancy grasped the swaying cable with her left arm. She was then slowly raised to the helicopter.

As she neared the top she looked down at what was left of the raft. It looked like a shrunken lemon with one end already sinking. Nancy shuddered to think what would have happened if the helicopter hadn't come.

Nancy felt an arm underneath hers, as a smiling man pulled her into the hovering craft. The cable was let down one more time to pick up the rescue swimmer. Nancy and Katie hugged each other in relief.

"Am I glad to see you guys," Nancy said to the rescuers. The pilot turned around and flashed a smile.

"Glad we could help," the man operating the cable said. "You're lucky to have friends who are concerned about you."

Nancy closed her eyes for a grateful moment. George and Bess! Thank goodness her friends had been thinking so clearly.

"We got a call from a George Fayne," the cable operator explained. "She said you were missing, and she had no idea where you might be. She was pretty frantic. She was worried the two of you might have been kidnapped. And then we heard from some fishermen who reported seeing a flare, and we put two and two together."

"We *were* kidnapped," Katie said. "Or I guess that's what you'd call it." She and Nancy explained what had happened to them.

"And you think this Jackie would actually go back and compete in the tournament as if nothing happened?" the pilot asked.

Katie shrugged. "Like Nancy said, if she's willing to do all this, then she must want to win pretty badly," she said.

"If we're lucky, we can make it back to the beach before she gets away," Nancy added, turning to the pilot.

"If it's an emergency, I can try to find an empty spot at Sand Harbor to land," he said.

In less than ten minutes Nancy saw the Sand Harbor shoreline come into view. To the right was the main beach area, filled with swimmers. To the left of the outcropping of rocks was the boat launch. A crowd of people were gathered at one end.

"The trick competition must have started," Katie said, peering through the helicopter's large window. The girls had now gathered behind the pilot, staring nervously at the crowded beach.

"And if I'm not mistaken, that's Jackie making her run now," Nancy said, pointing to the lone skier on the water. They all leaned forward to watch the skier sail across the water.

"That's her," Katie said, her anger returning. "And to think she pretended to be worried about me."

The pilot veered off to the left. "I'm going to land at the far end of the beach," he said. "There aren't any people there."

The helicopter swung in over the shoreline, hovering over an empty patch of sand on the beach. The pilot gently lowered the craft. "I won't be able to land here permanently," he said. "I'll just drop you off."

Nancy and Katie thanked their three rescuers.

The helicopter touched down, and the man who operated the cable opened the door. Nancy ducked and stepped out, looking toward the other end of the beach.

Jackie had just slid into a landing from her trick run. Standing in the shallow water, she popped her feet out of her skis. Then she saw the helicopter at the far end of the beach.

Jackie dropped her skis and began splashing out of the water and up the beach.

"Hurry!" Nancy yelled over her shoulder. "Jackie's escaping!"

15

Cut to the Chase

Nancy took off across the hot sand at a flat-out sprint. Figuring that Jackie would head for the parking lot, she turned up the beach, hoping to cut her off.

Nancy could hear shouts and exclamations of surprise as Jackie pushed her way through the crowd up the beach. Nancy hoped someone would stop her before she got away.

Katie caught up to Nancy and the two raced across the sand. Nancy held her right arm close to her body, trying not to move it.

"There she goes!" Katie suddenly yelled. Nancy saw Jackie burst out of the last group of people gathered on the beach. Out in the open now, Jackie was picking up speed.

Then Nancy saw another figure run out from the crowd. It was George! Nancy pointed at the fleeing Jackie. "Grab her!" she called to her friend.

With quick reflexes George began running up the beach after Jackie. About twenty yards away from the parking lot George lunged at the skier, grabbing her by the ankle. Jackie tumbled onto the sand, George still hanging on to her ankle.

Nancy and Katie rushed up to pin Jackie down as she frantically tried to twist out of George's grip.

"Get your hands off me!" Jackie spat out, kicking and squirming.

Nancy, George, and Katie held on tight. Jackie finally stopped thrashing around. The three girls hauled her to her feet. Several people had gathered around them, muttering questions.

"Let's head to the tent," Nancy suggested, motioning toward the large tournament tent.

Katie stood still, staring at the girl she had thought was her friend. "I don't get it," she said numbly to Jackie. "I—I . . ."

"Oh, you'll 'get it,' all right," Jackie snapped bitterly. "I'm sure little Miss Perfect will get everything she wants."

"And she'd deserve it after putting up with you," a deep voice behind Nancy said. She turned to see Mr. Cobb approaching them, followed by Mrs. Cobb. They both hurried over to hug Katie. "I'm so glad you are all right," Mrs. Cobb said, wiping tears from her eyes.

"Where were you?" Mr. Cobb asked.

"Out on the lake," Katie said. "We'll explain in a minute, but Nancy's hurt her arm. And I'm afraid I've missed the tournament."

"Margot Adler is skiing now," Mrs. Cobb said. "I'm sure when Pat McKiernan hears why you're late, he'll let you ski next. But only if you feel up to it."

Katie's eyes lit up. "I definitely want to give it a try," she said.

"Then let's go talk to Pat," Mrs. Cobb said. "Meanwhile, Nancy, we'll have the paramedics at the tent take a look at your shoulder." The mother and daughter team hurried down the beach.

Mr. Cobb yelled out to his daughter, "Good luck, honey. I know you can do it!" Nancy and George joined, shouting words of encouragement. "Go for it, Katie!"

Nancy, George, and Mr. Cobb led Jackie to the tent. "Now, can I finally find out what's been going on?" Katie's father asked as they moved along.

Just then Bess ran up to them. "Nancy, thank goodness you're all right," she said. Then she saw that Nancy and George were holding Jackie Albert. "What— I mean—it was—Jackie?" Bess stammered in confusion.

"Well said, cousin." George chuckled.

Nancy glanced at Jackie, but the skier's mouth

142

was drawn in a tight line, and she stared straight ahead. Nancy turned back to Bess. "Yes. It was Jackie. She knocked us unconscious and dumped us in a sinking raft in the lake."

Bess, George, and Mr. Cobb stared at Nancy, dumbfounded. Nancy went on. "I'm just glad the two of you called for a search helicopter when you did," she said.

George started to speak, but Mr. Cobb cut her off. "What kind of a maniac leaves two people stranded in the lake to die?" he barked at Jackie, his face contorted in anger. "And to lie to us for so long, too, pretending to support Katie, when—when . . ." He trailed off, unable to speak through his rage.

George turned to Nancy. "After we read your note we called the Cobbs and asked them for a ride to the beach. We ran into Katie's boat driver here. He said Jackie had met him earlier and told him they weren't going to practice. He left to get a cup of coffee and came back later."

Nancy nodded. "Jackie needed to use his boat, but she didn't want him in the way."

"Katie's car and our rental car were still in the parking lot, so we figured the two of you had been taken somewhere," George went on. "I thought a search would be faster by air than by foot, so I called the police who called the Tahoe Rescue Squad."

As the group reached the tent Pat McKiernan

ran over to meet them. "I just heard," he said. "Katie's on the lake now, taking her trick run."

"Oh, I'd better go watch," Mr. Cobb excused himself. He hurried away toward the water.

"I've called the police—they're on their way," McKiernan added, looking at Jackie in disbelief. "Whatever made you do such a thing?"

Jackie shrugged and dropped into a folding beach chair. She slumped down and stared out at the lake.

As a paramedic began to examine Nancy's arm, Nancy said, "She was probably thinking that as long as Katie was around, she'd never have a national title."

Jackie turned to her fiercely. "Oh, yes, I would have!" she said bitterly. "It would have been perfect. I'd switch to trick, Katie would stay with slalom, and I'd get the trick title. But, no," she said sarcastically. "Katie wasn't satisfied with one title. She needed them all." She was breathing heavily, consumed by anger.

"So you tried to remove Katie from the last day's competition?" McKiernan asked.

Jackie clamped her mouth shut and refused even to look at the director.

"That was only part of it," Nancy put in. "She was getting desperate because nothing else was working. At first she just tried to hurt Katie's performances. She moved the fin on Katie's slalom ski, so Katie fell during the first slalom run.

144

Then she jammed a pin in the release rope mechanism. It was only Tinker Clarkston's quick thinking that saved Katie from injury."

Nancy paused, wincing while the paramedic prodded her wrenched shoulder. "Jackie even tried to break into Katie's cabin, hoping to scare her with a warning note," Nancy continued. "And all along she was pretending to be Katie's friend and trying to blame Gary Trachok and Miller Burton for the sabotage.

"She even pretended to be helping me," Nancy continued. "She encouraged me to go to Truckee to check out Miller Burton. All she really wanted was to get us out of the way while she checked out the Cobbs' cabin.

"Then yesterday Jackie followed us to Donner Lake," she concluded. "She was trying to break into our car—maybe she planned to leave us stranded at the lake."

Just then an assistant ran into the tent, handing McKiernan a piece of paper. "Katie Cobb just had a great trick run," she said. "Here are the scores."

McKiernan glanced at the paper and raised his eyebrows, impressed. Picking up his bullhorn, he announced the scores. A cheer rose from the crowd, and Nancy and the others joined in.

Standing at the shore wrapped in a towel, Katie waved at her fans with a big grin.

"Oh, just perfect," Jackie muttered sarcastically from her chair. "Won't we all be excited when the princess collects another little crown?"

Nancy, Bess, and George all turned to Jackie. Though her impulse was to snap back at Jackie, there was something so scary about Jackie's hostility that Nancy didn't say a word.

A figure ducked into the shade of the tent, and Nancy saw it was Gary Trachok. The coach went straight to Pat McKiernan. "I just heard what happened," he said. "I'm glad Katie is all right."

Then Trachok saw Nancy. "I think I owe you an apology, Ms. Drew," he said. "That was me in the sailboat at the marina the night before last. I have to admit I was getting a little suspicious of your poking around, so I followed you out of the restaurant. I jumped in the first sailboat to watch you, when you picked the same boat to hide in, I panicked.

"I didn't mean to hit you with the boom," he added. "I thought it was tied down, but it swung away as I jumped out. I hope you're okay."

Nancy managed a smile. "It was just a bump," she said. "Nothing compared to this shoulder injury," she added with a grimace.

"Now that I've taped you up, it should heal pretty fast," the paramedic assured her.

After thanking the paramedic, Nancy turned back to Gary Trachok. "I'm still curious about something, Gary," she said. "You asked the owner of the ski shop in Truckee about adjusting ski fins. That seemed awfully coincidental, considering what caused Katie's first spill."

"I guess it was," Trachok considered. "But I knew Mike was an expert on this equipment. And we haven't been able to get Pam's ski right, so I wanted to run the problem by him."

"And how did you know the trick release was jammed?" Nancy asked.

"An educated guess," Trachok shrugged. "When I saw you checking out the release mechanism, I figured there were only two possibilities —an accident or an intentional jam. And I had seen Bridget fooling around with something in the boat."

As Pat McKiernan rejoined them Gary Trachok glanced over at Jackie and sighed. "I'm beginning to see what can happen if you get too wrapped up in skiing," he said. "I know Katie always felt I pushed her too hard. Maybe she was right. I guess people really can be pushed over the edge."

Pat McKiernan added, "Now Jackie will be eliminated from any tournament competition— not to mention the criminal charges she's going to face." He nodded toward two state police officers who were making their way toward the tent.

Nancy turned to her friends. "Let's go find the Cobbs," she suggested.

"Right," Bess said. "Katie should be ready to start her slalom run."

The girls walked down the beach to where Katie stood buckling on her life vest. Bridget kneeled beside her, rinsing sand from Katie's ski.

"Bridget seems a little happier today," Nancy commented softly to Mr. Cobb.

He nodded. "We had a long talk last night. She's right—we do spend a lot of time on Katie. We don't want Bridget to feel neglected."

The group watched Katie take off on her slalom run, picking up speed as she headed for the first buoy. "This is the most difficult run," Pat McKiernan said. "That rope is only thirty-nine feet long."

"What about the jump event?" George asked.

"The other three competitors have already jumped," McKiernan said. "And Katie's jump from the first day is still the highest. So if she does well on slalom, she'll win the tournament."

Nancy held her breath as she watched Katie work her way around the first buoys.

"Pam got through five buoys," Trachok said softly as he watched Katie swing around the fourth buoy. Though she had to stretch her body to make up for the shorter rope, each of Katie's movements was precise and studied.

When she made it around the sixth buoy, the crowd broke into applause. Katie seemed to realize she had done it, and her concentration broke. Her ski slid out from under her, and she fell with a loud splash. Nancy saw that Katie's arms were raised in victory as she surfaced.

"She did it!" Bess cried.

"All right!" George yelled.

Nancy saw Mr. and Mrs. Cobb and Bridget jumping up and down on shore, hugging one another and waving to Katie. Even Gary Trachok was clapping.

Nancy smiled as she watched Katie bob happily in the sparkling waters of Lake Tahoe. She knew this would be one tournament none of them would ever forget.

THE HARDY BOYS® SERIES By Franklin W. Dixon

NANCY DREW® MYSTERY STORIES By Carolyn Keene

BEAM ABOARD FOR NEW ADVENTURES!

A NEW TITLE EVERY OTHER MONTH!

Pocket Books presents a new, illustrated series for younger readers based on the hit television show:

Young Jake Sisko is looking for friends aboard the space station. He finds Nog, a Ferengi his own age, and together they find a whole lot of trouble!

#1: THE STAR GHOST
#2: STOWAWAYS
by Brad Strickland

#3: PRISONERS OF PEACE
by John Peel

#4: THE PET
by Mel Gilden and Ted Pedersen

#5: ARCADE
by Diana G. Gallagher

#6: FIELD TRIP
by John Peel

#7: GYPSY WORLD
by Ted Pedersen

Published by Pocket Books